The Babysitters Club

STACEY'S LIE

Ann M. Martin

Hippo

*The author gratefully acknowledges
Suzanne Weyn
for her help in
preparing this manuscript.*

Scholastic Children's Books,
Commonwealth House, 1–19 New Oxford Street,
London WC1A 1NU, UK
a division of Scholastic Ltd
London ~ New York ~ Toronto ~ Sydney ~ Auckland

First published in the USA by Scholastic Inc., 1994
First published in the UK by Scholastic Ltd, 1996

ISBN 0 590 13771 9

Typeset by Rowland Phototypesetting Ltd, Bury St Edmunds,
Suffolk
Printed by Cox & Wyman Ltd, Reading, Berks.

10 9 8 7 6 5 4 3 2 1

Are you following the Babysitters Club Mysteries series?

1 Stacey and the Missing Ring
2 Beware, Dawn!
3 Mallory and the Ghost Cat
4 Kristy and the Missing Child
5 Mary Anne and the Secret in the Attic
6 The Mystery at Claudia's House
7 Dawn and the Disappearing Dogs
8 Jessi and the Jewel Thieves
9 Kristy and the Haunted Mansion
10 Stacey and the Mystery Money
11 Claudia and the Mystery at the Museum
12 Dawn and the Surfer Ghost
13 Mary Anne and the Library Mystery
14 Stacey and the Mystery at the Mall
15 Kristy and the Vampires
16 Claudia and the Clue in the Photograph
17 Dawn and the Halloween Mystery
18 Stacey and the Mystery of the Empty House
19 Kristy and the Missing Fortune
20 Mary Anne and the Zoo Mystery

Look out for:

21 Claudia and the Recipe for Danger
22 Stacey and the Haunted Masquerade
23 Abby and the Secret Society

1st CHAPTER

"Yes, Dad, yes," I said, leaning against the kitchen wall and absent-mindedly wrapping the phone cord around my fingers. "No problem. Robert will understand. It's OK. You don't have to meet me at the information desk. I can just take a taxi from the station. Of course I remember where! Dad, please! I'm not a little kid! All right then, see you on Saturday. I love you too."

Just as I was ringing off, my mum walked in with a brown paper bag full of groceries. "Hi, Stacey," she said, putting the bag down on the table. She slipped off her beige blazer as she gave me a kiss on the cheek. "I'm exhausted. I had a hectic day at work. How was school?"

"Pretty good," I replied. "Nothing super-unusual."

1

"Who was on the phone?" she asked.

"Dad."

"Oh," Mum said in her I-will-betray-no-emotion voice. It's the flat voice she uses whenever we speak about my father. You see, Mum and Dad got divorced not long ago, and Dad isn't exactly Mum's favourite person on earth these days. But she tries not to show it, at least when she's with me. After all, I *am* still his daughter and I *do* love him. "What did he want?" she asked casually.

I began helping her put away the groceries. "There's been a slight change of plan. You know I was supposed to go and stay with him next weekend, but some business conference thing has come up, so he wanted to know if I could come *this* weekend instead. I told him it was no problem."

Mum sighed. "Nothing is more important to your father than work," she commented, annoyance working its way into her voice.

"It's no big deal, Mum," I said. "Robert and I were just going to go and see a film. We can go next weekend."

Robert is my steady boyfriend. I'm crazy about him. He's a really great guy. And he understands why I spend lots of weekends in New York City with my

2

father. I was pretty sure he wouldn't mind this little adjustment.

"Anyway, this change of plan solves one problem," I said. "Sunday is Father's Day. I've been wondering how I would get Dad's present to him. I could have posted it, but I've already waited too long. Now I'll be able to give it to him."

"I wonder if that's why your father changed the date," Mum said thoughtfully. "So you could be with him on Father's Day."

"Wouldn't he have just come out and said so?" I asked as I ripped open a bag of sliced carrots.

"Your father's funny when it comes to sentimental things like that," Mum said, covering her cream-coloured silk shirt and matching slacks with a purple-and-gold-striped apron. "Even though he might want you with him on Father's Day, he probably wouldn't just come out and admit it."

"Why not?" I asked.

"Some people have trouble talking about their emotions," she said as she tore the wrapping off a packet of chicken pieces. "Your father's definitely one of those people."

I thought about that. To me, Dad seems OK about emotions. I've never wondered whether he's glad to see me or not – he always gives me a big hug. I know he loves me. "What kind of emotions can't he talk about?" I asked.

Mum picked up her favourite knife and started slicing the skin off the chicken. "He doesn't like to show his softer side. And he doesn't like to discuss anything that might possibly get the other person upset. He'd rather just avoid talking about difficult things altogether."

I thought of the terrible shouting fights Mum and Dad had had just before they told me they were getting divorced. Naturally, both of them had been very upset (not to mention how *I* felt, sitting in my room listening to them). But if Dad really didn't like talking about emotional, upsetting things, it must have been murder on him.

"Homework calls," I said to Mum, giving her a kiss on the cheek. I picked up a carrot stick and went upstairs.

I never really mind maths homework. We're doing some pre-algebra work. I love it! Algebra is so balanced and logical. Maths is my absolute favourite subject.

When my last homework problem was done, I went back downstairs. On the way, I could smell the tarragon-lemon chicken cooking. It smelled great. It made me want to eat, even though I wasn't really that hungry right then.

It's a good thing Mum makes really great meals because whether I'm hungry or not, I have to eat supper. I can't afford to skip a meal or let myself get too hungry. That's because I have diabetes.

Diabetes is a condition which prevents my body from regulating the amount of sugar in my blood. In order to keep it under control I have to eat a healthy, carefully balanced diet. So, even though I eat snacks, I can't eat just anything I want. Unlike a lot of my friends I don't snack on sweets or junk food. (My best friend, Claudia, eats so many junk food snacks that I don't know how she manages to eat supper at all! I'll tell you more about her later.)

I have to take my diabetes very seriously. Cheating on my diet could send me into a diabetic coma – which is as awful as it sounds. I also have to give myself insulin injections every day.

Every once in a while I feel sorry for myself about the diabetes. But I usually snap out of it pretty quickly. The disease rarely stops me from doing anything I want to do. And I'm not one for self-pity. My attitude is that life goes on and you have to keep looking for the good in it.

When Mum and I sat down to dinner

5

(which tasted as good as it smelled), we had a lot to talk about. She's a buyer for Bellair's department store. That means she decides which items the shop will sell. Today she'd had a huge problem at work. A line of winter coats she'd ordered came in and they were all wrong. (As it's June I can't imagine even *looking* at a winter coat! But department stores order their stuff a long time ahead of the season.) The coats were supposed to be in a selection of black, red and blue. Instead the coats that came in were fake fur in a selection of zebra-striped, leopard-spotted or tiger-striped. (Which sounded pretty cool to me, but it wasn't what Mum thought the people who shop in Bellair's would want to buy.) She'd spent the whole day on the phone arguing with the coat company.

Mum shook her head as she scooped up a forkful of peas. "Sometimes I wonder why I was so keen to work."

Mum didn't work full-time till after the divorce. But now she loves her job (most days). And I'm happier because the job distracts her from me. Mum used to spend a lot of time worrying about me, mostly because of my diabetes. Now, I suppose she still worries, but she has other things to think about, too.

6

The next morning I got up, pulled on a pair of blue tights, black denim shorts, a long-sleeved blue T-shirt, and a pair of black flat shoes. I piled my blonde permed hair up on top of my head and fastened it with a blue scrunchie.

Then I looked out of my bedroom window and realized my outfit was all wrong. Those weren't tiny green buds on the trees any more – they were actual leaves. And the sky was blue and clear. It looked much more like summer than spring. I opened the window. A warm breeze was blowing. It changed my mood entirely.

I ripped the scrunchie out of my hair and let the curls fall around my shoulders. I took off my clothes and changed into my new one-piece shorts dress with the gold, red and green Aztec-style print. I slipped on a pair of light tan fabric shoes and I was ready to go.

The change of clothes had put me a little behind schedule. But I quickly gulped down a bowl of Shredded Wheat (plain, no sugar) and a glass of orange juice. Skipping breakfast is a no-no for me. "Looks like we're both running late today," said Mum as she came into the kitchen, still tying the bow on her blouse.

7

"Did you change outfits at the last minute too?" I asked with a laugh.

Mum laughed with me. "Yes, I did," she admitted. "I couldn't wear a black gabardine trouser suit on a day like today. It's gorgeous outside."

"Summer at last," I said as I kissed her cheek and went out of the door.

"Have a good day," she called after me.

I half walked, half ran to the corner of Elm Street. I live at 89 Elm Street. This is my second Stoneybrook address. I used to live at 612 Fawcett Avenue, but my friend Jessi lives there now.

Maybe I should explain. At the beginning of seventh grade, we moved from New York City, where I grew up, to Stoneybrook, because my father's company transferred him here. Then – just when I'd made friends and had begun to feel at home – the company transferred him back to the city. *Then* my parents decided to get divorced, and my mother made plans to move back to Stoneybrook. I had to choose where I wanted to live. That was such a difficult choice! But what helped me decide was how much I missed my friends here in Stoneybrook.

So I came back to Stoneybrook with Mum. It was the right choice. If I'd stayed

8

in the city, I would never have been able to take back my job as treasurer of the BSC.

BSC stands for Babysitters Club. Claudia, my best friend, is in it too, and so are several other good friends. I'll tell you more about the BSC later.

My friends Mary Anne and Mallory were waiting for me at the corner of Elm Street and Bradford Court. (Some mornings I run through my back garden and into Mal's, and leave with her. Other mornings – like this one – I'm running too late to do that.) As we made our way towards Stoneybrook Middle School, we stopped at my old house and picked up our other friend, Jessi.

When I got to school, Robert was waiting at my locker. Even though I'd seen Robert just the day before, my heart still began to race when I caught sight of him. As I said, I'm crazy about him. He isn't exactly model-gorgeous like, say, Jason Priestly, but to me he's simply adorable. He's got dark brown hair, deep, dark eyes, and broad shoulders. "Hi, Stace," he said with a smile. (His smile just finishes me off! It makes me melt, completely. Did I mention his dimples?)

"Hi," I said, smiling back.

Then a funny thing happened. "Guess

9

what?" we both said at once, which cracked us up.

"You go first," I said.

"OK," said Robert. He looked pretty excited about whatever he was preparing to say. "Remember I told you that my family always spends the holidays at our house in Davis Park?"

I nodded. "On Fire Island. Don't remind me. You'll be there for the whole of August with your family."

The smile faded from Robert's face. "That's the only bad part about it."

"About what?"

"My summer job."

"You've got a summer job!" I cried happily. I knew how much Robert had been hoping to land one. "What will you be doing?"

Robert folded his arms and leaned against my locker. "It's a great job. Dad's friend knows the people who run the ferry between Long Island and Davis Park. He got me a job working on the boat for two months this summer."

"Excellent!" I cried. Then I frowned. "Wait a minute. Not excellent. When does this job start?"

"Next weekend."

"What?" I cried. "You mean as soon as school ends, you have to go?"

10

Robert nodded. "Until my family comes out in August I'll stay with my father's friend's family. I'll see my family pretty often anyway – they'll come out for weekends in July, too."

"This is terrible," I said with a sigh.

Robert took my hand. "It's really just a month longer, as I'd be gone for August anyway. And you'd probably be in the city for two of the weekends in July. If I were staying at home I'd have to get a job during the week. So all we're losing is two weekends, when you think about it."

"It's OK," I said glumly. "I mean, it's not OK. But I understand."

"At least we've got this weekend," he said.

"No, we haven't," I said, shaking my head. "That's what I was going to tell you. My father asked me if I could come and see him this weekend instead of next, and I said yes."

"But by next weekend I'll be gone," Robert pointed out.

"I know," I said. Maybe I could skip seeing my father this weekend. That would mean I wouldn't see him for three whole weeks, though. And this was Father's Day weekend. I couldn't cancel my visit to him for Father's Day. Could I?

11

2nd CHAPTER

I stepped out of the train late that Friday afternoon and joined the flow of people moving up the platform towards the main lobby of Grand Central Station. Yes, Grand Central, in New York City. Of course, I hadn't cancelled my weekend with my father. How could I, on Father's Day weekend?

So there I was, being swept along with the crowd. All the way down on the train, I'd sat slumped in my seat and thought about Robert. Last weekend we'd played ping-pong at the Stoneybrook Community Centre games room, then browsed around the crafts fair outside, where I'd found a great Father's Day present for Dad. Then we'd ridden our bikes into town and had lunch. It was a great day. A perfect day! On the way back home,

12

we'd stopped our bikes at the end of Bradford Court. Robert had reached over and given me the most wonderful kiss.

As I said, everything was perfect. But I hadn't known it would be our last full day together for the whole summer! I don't know if I would have done anything differently, but I do wish I'd known.

As rotten as I felt about Robert going away, a different feeling took over as I stepped out of the train tunnel and into Grand Central Station's beautiful lobby with its high, domed ceiling.

My mood began to lift. My pulse quickened as the excitement of being back in New York City took hold of me.

New York is *so* different from Stoneybrook. I love both places, but there's just nothing like the Big Apple. It's louder, brighter, faster. It's packed out with museums, shops, restaurants, great buildings . . . and people. In the city you see people from all over the world – rich, poor, and every colour, shape and size. And all of them seem to be rushing somewhere. Especially on a Friday afternoon!

I adjusted my heavy canvas overnight bag on my shoulder and crossed the lobby, heading for the door that leads to the taxi ranks. My bag dug into my

13

shoulder. I had packed too much stuff (as usual), and I had Dad's Father's Day present with me too. As I passed the information desk, someone called my name. I turned sharply. There was Dad, rushing towards me.

"Dad!" I cried happily, putting down my bag. He wrapped me in a hug. It was so good to see him.

"But Dad, you weren't supposed to meet me," I reminded him.

"I know," he said as he picked up my suitcase. "But I just couldn't resist it."

"Aren't you supposed to be working?" I noticed he was dressed casually, in khaki slacks and a striped sports shirt. He always wears suits to work.

"I took a work-at-home day," he said. "Sometimes it's easier to get work done without all the interruptions and distractions of the office."

We started walking up the ramp to the side of the station where taxis wait. "See how easy this is?" I said. "I would have walked up this ramp, got into a taxi, and gone right to the front of your building. I'd have been perfectly safe."

"So, I'm a hopeless worrier," he said with a laugh. He put his hand on my shoulder. "But you're my girl. I'm not

14

taking any chances with your safety. You're too precious to me."

I smiled at him. Secretly, I was glad he'd come. Although I wanted to be independent, I also liked being cared for. It made me feel warm inside. At that moment, I knew I had done the right thing by not cancelling this weekend.

We got a taxi quickly. Dad gave a fake groan as he dropped my bag on the seat. "What did you pack? Bricks?"

I smiled mysteriously. His guess was pretty close. Actually, it was marble. At the crafts fair, there was a man selling beautiful marble chess sets. The playing pieces were sculpted into figures from the armies of the Civil War. Dad loves chess and he loves history, so it was the perfect gift for him. The set had cost me most of the babysitting money I'd saved up over the spring, but it was worth it. It was pretty heavy, though. Carrying it home in my bicycle basket had been tricky.

Soon the taxi turned into East 65th Street, and pulled up in front of Dad's building. His flat is really cool. It's old and classy, with lovely brick walls inside and a cosy little fireplace. My bedroom there is a bit on the small side, but as I don't spend all that much time in it, I really don't mind.

15

"Stace, I need to ask you a favour," Dad said as we put my bags down inside the flat. "Can you give me a couple of hours to finish off some work?"

"Do you have to go into the office?" I wailed.

"No, it's not that bad. Remember? I'm set up at home now." He pointed to the desk by the window. It used to be cluttered with papers. Now it was set up with a computer, a printer and a fax machine.

"I see," I said glumly. "Now you can work *all* the time, day or night, at home or in the office."

"No, no, this is a good thing," Dad insisted. "It means I don't have to be in the office so much. It gives me a lot more free time. Really."

Yes, I thought. More free time to work. If I was missing my last weekend with Robert just so that I could sit here and watch him work all weekend, I was going to be really annoyed.

The expression on my face must have told Dad I was fuming. "Stacey, honestly, give me these few hours and you won't be sorry. I've got a little surprise lined up, but if I don't take this time I can't make it happen."

"What kind of surprise?" I asked.

16

"You'll see." It was his turn to smile mysteriously. He took his wallet out of his back pocket. "How would you like to go and buy yourself a pretty, summery something to wear to dinner tonight? I'll take you to the Lion's Lair." He handed me some money.

So much for pouting. I gave Dad a kiss and was out of the door before he'd even turned on his computer. There are loads of small boutiques and clothes shops in his neighbourhood, packed with styles that haven't quite made it to Stoneybrook or Washington Mall yet. This was going to be fun.

After an hour or so of looking around, I settled for this super flowing trouser suit in a sunflower print on a navy blue background. It had a high waist, cap sleeves and a scooped neckline, and the trousers were long and full. I loved it. I had a few dollars left over, so I stopped at the market on the corner and looked at all the bright flowers in buckets out at the front. At last I settled for four tall sunflowers. (I'm on a bit of a sunflower kick these days.)

Back upstairs, I could hear a high whining sound, followed by several clicks, as I knocked on Dad's door. "What's that?" I asked, as he let me in.

"It's the sound of my fax machine,

sending a ten-page report to a client in Washington DC."

"Wow! And I thought overnight mail was fast," I commented. I handed him the sunflowers. "An early Father's Day gift."

"Thanks. Is Father's Day soon?" Dad asked with a twinkle in his eyes.

I punched his arm playfully. "You know it's on Sunday."

Dad smiled and handed the flowers back to me. "Would you put these in water for me? I want to have a shower, and then we can go out to eat." I found a vase under his sink and put the flowers in it. They looked great on the small round table in the corner of the flat.

By seven-thirty I was dressed in my new outfit and waiting for Dad. He was on the phone, talking to a client in California. (It was only four-thirty out there.) "That's the great thing about California," Dad said as he rang off. "You can phone in the evening, and everybody's still in the office. You can really stretch your working day that way."

Leave it to my dad to find a way to stretch his working day!

Talking about California made me think of my good friend Dawn, who's in California now. She's another BSC

18

member. Like me, her parents are divorced. And like me, she's with her father at the moment. (Dawn grew up in California; she and her mother came to Stoneybrook after the divorce.) Dawn says she's just there to visit her dad and her brother, Jeff, who lives with her father. My friends and I are all worried that she might decide to stay there. Dawn's got California in her blood, just the way I have New York City in mine.

"Ready?" Dad asked at last.

"Ready," I replied, picking up my bag. We went downstairs and out on to the dusky street. I love this time of day in the city, when the sun is setting. People are home from their jobs, and getting ready to go out again. The traffic is less heavy, and a kind of temporary quietness falls over everything. Quiet for the city, that is. There are still sirens in the background, the low rumble of the subway below ground, the occasional helicopter *chop-chop-chopping* above you. But somehow the volume seems a little lower. I think the sharp edges of the tall buildings even look softer.

We walked up several blocks towards the Lion's Lair, on 70th Street. "How are you and Robert doing these days?" Dad asked.

"Great," I said. "Only he's going to be away most of the summer." I decided not to go into any details. I didn't want Dad to feel bad about my missing my last weekend with Robert.

"That's a shame," said Dad. "But maybe it's a good thing for you two to spend the summer apart."

My hands went to my hips. "Why?" I asked indignantly.

"You're both young. It's not good to become too involved with one person at your age. Maybe this summer you'll meet someone you like better than Robert."

"Better than Robert? No way!" I cried.

Dad laughed. "OK, OK. I suppose it must be true love. I'm just an old dad and I don't want to lose my girl to some guy called Robert. At least not so soon."

I took hold of his arm and leaned my head against it. "You'll never lose me, Dad. That's impossible."

By the time we got to the Lion's Lair, it was nearly dark. Outside, they'd turned on all these tiny, twinkly white lights. We walked down the stone steps into the restaurant. A hostess in a lovely red silk suit greeted us. "I've made a reservation," Dad told her. "Ed McGill."

"We've opened our outdoor seating

20

today," the hostess told him. "Would you like to sit there or inside?"

Dad looked at me. "Outside sounds great," I said. We followed her through the restaurant, which was decorated with sculptures of lions and big stone lion heads which jutted out from the brick walls. She pushed open a sliding glass door and we stepped outside on to a patio. Right next to the patio was a huge rock ledge. All around and above us the windows in blocks of flats were beginning to light up. The patio was like a little bit of country protected by the rock.

When the waiter came, I ordered shrimp cocktail (which, for me, amounts to shrimp on ice, as I can't eat the cocktail sauce) and boiled red snapper. Dad asked for raw oysters to start and steak *au poivre* (that's French for "with peppercorns") and handed the menus back to the waiter.

"Ready for my surprise?" Dad asked.

"Yes," I replied.

"Remember that conference I told you about – the one scheduled for next week? Well, I was informed just today that I would *not* have to attend after all. As long as the client receives my report by Monday, she could present my study and conclusions at the conference. That's why I was so determined to finish it today."

21

Was Dad expecting me to jump up and down? I mean, this wasn't exactly a wonderful surprise. In fact, it meant I could have come to the city next weekend after all, and not missed this last weekend with Robert.

"That's not the surprise," Dad went on. "The surprise is this: I've decided to take a two-week holiday, starting next weekend. My appointment calendar is clear for that time, as I thought I'd be at the conference. It's a perfect time for me to go away. I'd like you to come with me, Stacey."

Now that *was* a surprise! "Great!" I cried. "Where are we going?"

"You name it. Anywhere you want. I'm leaving it completely up to you. We could go out west, or up to the mountains for two weeks. How about Disney World? Or are you too old for that? Maybe Europe? What do you think?"

This was astounding! *My* father, the workaholic, was actually going to take two whole weeks off? He'd hardly ever taken that much time off. Sometimes my mother and I had gone away together and he'd joined us at the end of the week. Or we'd all go away together, and he'd leave early. "Are you sure you can handle two weeks off?" I asked.

22

"No," he said with a smile. "But I'm going to do it anyway. So, where are we going?"

"I don't know," I said. This was a big decision. "Can I have till Sunday to think about it?"

"Of course," Dad agreed.

"I suppose I ought to phone Mum and check with her," I added.

"Good idea," Dad agreed. "But I bet it will be fine."

When my food came it tasted extra delicious. I wasn't sure if it was the food or that I was feeling so happy.

My happy mood continued through Saturday. It was another beautiful, warm day. Dad and I went to the Museum of Natural History, which I've always loved. We saw the new, expanded dinosaur exhibition, which was pretty cool, and we looked at the star show at the Planetarium. After that, Dad took me to this huge CD and tape shop near Lincoln Center. We spent over an hour there. Then we went to Chinatown for supper, and back to the West Village to see a play.

That night, I lay in the dark in my tiny bedroom and watched the car lights from the street outside gliding across the ceiling. Physically I was exhausted, but my mind was wide awake. I couldn't stop thinking about where Dad and I should go on our holiday.

I didn't feel too old for Disney World but I'd been there already (on this great trip with the BSC). Maybe it was time for a trip to Europe. Would two weeks be long enough? Or should I come up with something closer to home?

Europe sounded good, though. I put my hands behind my head and pictured myself sitting in a smart little café on a Parisian boulevard. I'd wear a great red beret with something super stylish. As elegant Parisians walked past, I'd bend my head close to the person sitting beside me to say something very clever in French.

No. There was a problem with that picture. The person I pictured beside me at the table was Robert, *not* my father. Maybe it would be better to go somewhere else with Dad and save the European trip for some other time. (Like a honeymoon with Robert. Who knows? It could happen.)

I sat up, leaning on my elbows. I'd had a great idea! I could go to California and visit Dawn. California isn't really much closer than Europe, but I'd get to see Dawn.

I lay back down and shut my eyes. In

24

the morning I'd tell Dad what I'd decided. We were California bound!

After that, sleep came pretty fast. Soon I was dreaming. Dawn and I were surfing, riding perfect wave after perfect wave. Then the dream changed. I was with Robert on a sailing boat. The sky was clear and the wind filled the sail. In my dream, the boat was sailing itself, while we sat with our arms around each other.

It was the most romantic dream.

When I opened my eyes, Dad was already moving around the flat. "Morning," he greeted me as I shuffled into the kitchen.

"Good morning," I said sleepily, sitting down at the table. Suddenly, I remembered my dream. "Dad," I said. "I've decided where I want to go on holiday."

"Where?" he asked.

"Davis Park," I said. (Sorry, Dawn.)

3rd CHAPTER

On Monday I could hardly wait to tell my friends my holiday news, but I decided to put it off till our BSC meeting at 5:30. That way I could tell them all at once.

At first, Dad had been surprised by my choice. He knew about Davis Park, but hadn't expected that I would. I told him I'd heard about it from friends, but I didn't mention Robert. I didn't want to hurt his feelings. He might think I wasn't interested in spending time with him – that the only reason I wanted to go to Davis Park was because of Robert. That wasn't *exactly* true. Robert would be at work all day, and I *would* be spending time with my father. But by going to Davis Park, I'd be able to see Robert some of the time, which was certainly better than seeing him *none* of the time.

26

Anyway, at breakfast that day Dad said he thought going to Davis Park was a great idea. When we'd eaten, I gave him his Father's Day gift. He loved the chess set as much as I'd hoped. "I'll teach you to play on the beach at Davis Park," Dad said happily.

I arrived at Claudia's house before 5:30 on Monday and let myself in. (The Kishis don't mind – they're used to the BSC members trooping in and out on meeting days. We've always met there.) I bounded up the stairs. "Hi, Claud," I said as I walked into her bedroom and bounced on to her bed.

"Hi," said Claudia, putting down her sketchbook. She had been drawing with coloured pencils, and her picture looked a bit like a cartoon. It was a group portrait of the BSC members.

"This is excellent," I said, looking more closely. "My hair isn't that curly, though."

"It's a caricature," Claudia explained. "Everything's supposed to be a bit exaggerated."

The cartoon – or caricature – really was good. Claudia's such a talented artist. She sculpts, does pottery and silk-screening, makes jewellery, paints. You name it! If it's artistic, Claudia does it, and does it well.

As I mentioned, Claudia is my very best friend. She's really beautiful, with long, silky black hair and absolutely perfect skin. She's Japanese-American, and has the most gorgeous, dark, almond-shaped eyes.

She also has a fabulous sense of style. Like me, Claudia's really into fashion, but she does everything her own way. Claudia knows how to personalize a look. She'll combine clothing in a way you might think would be disastrous, and instead of disaster she ends up with perfection. For example, today she was wearing a black, knee-length crocheted jacket over a pair of black shorts and a white blouse with ruffles at the collar and cuffs. Her hair was in two long plaits tied with black and white ribbons at the ends. On her feet were black sandals with a thick plat-form sole and white ribbons laced around her ankles. (The ribbons had originally been black, but Claudia had cut them off and glued on white ribbons.) The outfit might sound crazy, but it looked great!

"Claudia," I said. "I've got to talk to you about something."

Claudia fished a big packet of Mini Cheddars from behind her pillow. (Claudia has to hide all her junk food because her parents don't approve at all.)

"What?" she asked as she tore open the bag.

"Would you like to come to Davis Park, on Fire Island, for two weeks with Dad and me?" Dad had told me I could bring her if she wanted to come. He said it would be good if I had some company in case he had to catch up on a little work while we were there. (That's my dad the workaholic for you. I suppose I couldn't expect him to change *completely*.)

Claudia dropped her Mini Cheddars all over the bed. "Of course I would!" she cried. "That would be great! When?"

"We'd travel down to the city after school this Friday. Dad would meet us. Then we'd take the train out to Long Island early on Saturday morning and take the ferry over."

"Friday will be my lucky day," said Claudia happily. "The last day of school *and* a trip to Fire Island." Claudia isn't very keen on school. She's bright but she's not good at academic things, she's a horrible speller, and she doesn't care about grades. She just wants to do well enough to keep her parents from getting too upset.

Mr and Mrs Kishi aren't very pleased about Claudia's attitude to school. Claudia's older sister, Janine, is a real high-IQ genius. She already takes college

29

classes even though she's still at high school. I suppose the Kishis expected Claudia to follow in Janine's footsteps. Lately, it seems they've been appreciating Claudia's own strengths a little more.

"I'll have to ask Mum and Dad, of course," said Claudia, picking up the Mini Cheddars. "But I'm sure they'll say yes. Why did you choose Davis Park? Isn't that where Robert's family has a house?"

"That's right. Robert's family spends every August there and he makes it sound so nice," I said. Somehow, I just couldn't bring myself to tell her the whole story, about Robert getting the job on the ferry and all. I hadn't told anyone about Robert going away so soon, I suppose because I'd felt too sad to talk about it. Now I decided not to tell Claudia because I was afraid she wouldn't want to come if she knew Robert would be there. She might think she'd be a gooseberry. That wasn't true, though. Robert would be working most of the time.

"Too bad you can't go in August, when Robert will be there," Claudia said. "But it's good for me. If Robert were there you wouldn't need me to come along."

"I'd still want you there," I insisted.

"No, you wouldn't," she said with a wave of her hand. "I'd just be in the way."

30

That did it. Once she said that, I knew I'd been right not to tell her about Robert.

"Hi, you two." Claudia and I looked up to see Kristy Thomas coming through the door. As usual, she was dressed in jeans, a T-shirt and trainers, and her long brown hair was pulled back in a ponytail. She sat down in Claudia's director's chair, which is where she always sits during BSC meetings. Reaching over, she picked Claudia's sketch up off the bed. "Hey, this is great," she said. "Only, I'm not *that* short."

"It's a caricature," Claudia explained again. "Everything is exaggerated."

"Yes, but you've made me the shortest one in the group," she protested.

"You *are* the shortest one," Claudia reminded her.

"Even shorter than Mary Anne?" she asked.

Claudia and I both nodded. Kristy frowned and studied the picture. "You know, this picture gives me an idea," she said, almost as if she were talking to herself.

Claudia and I exchanged a Look. Something is *always* giving Kristy an idea. Great ideas are what she's famous for. In fact, the Babysitters Club was Kristy's idea to begin with.

31

It came to her one day when her mother was trying to get a babysitter for her younger brother, David Michael. Kristy and her two older brothers, Sam and Charlie, were all going to be busy the following afternoon when Mrs Thomas needed a sitter. And Kristy's father had left the family shortly after David Michael was born, so obviously *he* couldn't babysit either.

Her mother seemed to be making a trillion phone calls without finding anyone to sit. That's when it occurred to Kristy that parents would love being able to phone one number and reach several babysitters all at once.

Kristy told her great idea to her best friend Mary Anne Spier. They told Claudia, and Claud suggested inviting me to be part of the Babysitters Club, too.

We put up posters advertising our new babysitting service. Parents could call Claudia's private phone number between 5:30 and 6:00 every Monday, Wednesday and Friday and reach four qualified babysitters. It was an instant success. Straight away we had more business than we could handle.

We were so swamped that Mary Anne suggested we invite Dawn Schafer to join the group. Dawn was new in school; Mary

Anne had just met her, but they'd hit it off straight away.

As I've told you, Dawn's from California. She's tall and slim, with long, white-blonde hair. Her style of dressing is casual but cool. And Dawn is very much her own person. She cares deeply about social causes and the environment, for example. And even when it isn't easy, she follows her own beliefs.

It was funny that Mary Anne and Dawn became such instant friends, partly because Mary Anne's incredibly shy, and partly because at first glance, Dawn and Mary Anne seem pretty different. Mary Anne is short (though not quite as short as Kristy), she's on the quiet side, and she has brown hair and brown eyes. When Mary Anne met Dawn she was still wearing her hair in plaits every day and dressing in pinafore dresses and long socks. (Her clothes and hair weren't entirely her fault. Her father was still super-strict in those days.)

Not long after they met, Dawn and Mary Anne became more than good friends. They became stepsisters! Unbelievable but true! Looking through Mrs Schafer's old high school yearbook, they found out that she and Mr Spier had once been boyfriend and girlfriend. Things

33

hadn't worked out then, but now Mrs Schafer was divorced and Mr Spier was a widower (Mary Anne's mother died when Mary Anne was small) so they had a second chance. And Mary Anne and Dawn were going to see that they made the most of it. It took some conniving to get their parents out on a date, but they did it. And, what seemed like a trillion dates later, Dawn's mother married Mary Anne's father.

They all moved into Dawn's cool old (built in 1795!) farmhouse on Burnt Hill Road. (The house has a real secret passage which runs from Dawn's room to the barn at the back of the house. It was once a stop on the Underground Railroad which helped escaped slaves flee from the South to Canada.)

At first, Dawn and Mary Anne were thrilled to be stepsisters. But then they found that becoming a family wasn't as easy as they'd thought. The first big new-family crisis was over food. Dawn and her mother eat health food like tofu and bean-curd, and no red meat. Mary Anne and her father eat ordinary food. They couldn't even get a meal together without half the family being revolted by what the other half of the family was eating.

There were all sort of little problems

along the way. But now they seem to be working everything out all right. Mary Anne's father relaxed some of his rules enough so that Mary Anne could start dressing more her age. He even went along with it when she got her hair cut into a cute, short style.

Things were going so well that it was quite a surprise when Dawn announced recently that she wanted to go to California to spend some time with Jeff and her dad. Mary Anne tries to understand (she's a very sensitive and understanding person), but I know she misses Dawn a lot.

Anyway, back to BSC history: there we were with a five-member club, when I got the big news that my family would be moving back to New York City. While I was away, the club took on two new members, Mallory (Mal) Pike and Jessi Ramsey. Both girls are eleven and in the sixth grade (and they happen to be best friends). Because of their age they're junior officers. Basically that means they can only sit in the daytime, unless they're looking after their own siblings. Still, what they do frees us older members (the rest of us are thirteen) to take on more jobs.

Like me, Jessi came to Stoneybrook because her father was transferred here.

As I mentioned, she moved right into my old house. She's originally from Oakley, New Jersey. Her neighbourhood there was comfortably integrated – there were probably more black families on her block than there are in the whole of Stoneybrook. (Oh, did I say that Jessi is African-American? Well, she is.) Anyway, at first some of their new Stoneybrook neighbours let the Ramseys know they weren't pleased about an African-American family moving in. This was Jessi's first encounter with prejudice, and it was miserable. But her family stuck it out, and now they feel at home here. They've got good friends and neighbours.

Jessi's family consists of her parents, herself (of course), her sister Becca (who's eight), and her little brother, Squirt, who's two. (His real name is John Philip, Jr.) Also her aunt Cecelia, who came to live with them when Mrs Ramsey went back to work.

Jessi is a very talented ballet dancer. She goes to lessons in Stamford, which is the closest city to Stoneybrook. She's already appeared in several professional productions. I'm sure she'll go on to be a real star.

I think Mallory might grow up to be famous, too. But not as a ballerina, as an

36

author. Mal wants to write and illustrate children's books. One of her stories has already won an award in a school competition.

Mal has everything she needs to be a successful children's book author. She has a good sense of humour, a nice way with words, a great imagination, and she knows kids really well. That's because she's the oldest of eight! After Mal come the ten-year-old triplets, Adam, Byron and Jordan; Vanessa (nine); Nicky (eight); Margo (seven); and lastly, Claire, who is five.

Mal has curly brown hair with reddish highlights. She wears glasses and a brace, and she hates her nose. Mal doesn't think she's pretty, but I bet she'll be a knockout one of these days. I don't think her nose is so awful, for a start. One day she can get contact lenses (her parents say she's too young now), and eventually the brace will come off. Mal can't wait.

I glanced over at Claudia's caricature. Mal even looked cute in that.

As I looked at the sketch my eye fell on the picture of Shannon Kilbourne, who was standing next to Mal in the picture. Shannon is the newest member of the BSC. And as I was studying Claud's sketch of Shannon to see if it was a true

37

resemblance, she walked in the door.

"Great! I'm on time!" cheered Shannon as she came into the room.

I glanced at Claudia's digital clock. It was 5:26. Kristy, who is the club chairman, is very strict about punctuality. But Shannon's hardly ever late; she's Kristy's neighbour and they usually arrive together. "I had a rehearsal at school today," she explained. "I'm in a comedy sketch the honour society is doing at the end-of-term assembly."

Shannon doesn't go to Stoneybrook Middle School like the rest of us. She attends Stoneybrook Day School, a private school at the other end of town.

That might sound snobby, but Shannon's no snob. She's really nice. Actually, Kristy thought she was a snob when she first met her. But that had more to do with Kristy's adjusting to her new, wealthy neighbourhood than it had to do with Shannon.

Kristy used to live on Bradford Court, opposite the Kishis. Then her mother married this man called Watson Brewer. After the wedding, the Thomas family all moved to the other side of town to a much smarter area of Stoneybrook where Watson's mansion was located. That's

38

right, I said *mansion*! Watson just happens to be a millionaire.

Mansion or not, Kristy wasn't happy about the move at first. (She's not the kind of person to be impressed by things like mansions. She's the most down-to-earth person I've ever met.) She felt a bit cut off from the rest of us. But soon we came up with the idea of paying her older brother Charlie to drive her to BSC meetings. And after a while she got to like Watson. Also, she adores Watson's kids from his first marriage, Karen (seven) and Andrew (four), and they adore her. They spend every other month with Watson. Kristy also gained another younger sister when Watson and her mother adopted a little Vietnamese girl they called Emily Michelle. She's two and a half now.

Anyway, Shannon's house is right opposite Watson's, and that's how Kristy met Shannon. At first, Shannon was just an associate BSC member. She didn't come to meetings, but we rang her if we were offered a job that none of us could take. With Dawn in California, Shannon has started coming to meetings regularly. The more we get to know her, the more we like her. She's bright, cute (curly blonde hair, big blue eyes), funny and friendly. She's got two younger sisters,

Tiffany and Maria, and a Bernese mountain dog called Astrid of Grenville.

We do still have one associate member. He's Mary Anne's boyfriend, Logan Bruno. Logan is originally from Kentucky and has the cutest southern drawl. He and Mary Anne are very close.

By 5:30, everyone was in the room. "OK, let's get started," Kristy said in her usual no-nonsense way. "Stacey, what's our treasury like at the moment?"

"Well, it's Monday, subs day. When everyone's paid, I think we'll be in good shape," I reported. We all have official titles and jobs. (Actually, Mal and Jessie have titles, but no duties.) As you may have guessed, I'm the treasurer. I fished a manila envelope out of my school rucksack. It holds our subs. I collect subs each week and then try to spend the money as carefully as possible. "We've paid Charlie for this month. And we paid the monthly standard charge on Claudia's phone bill last week."

Claudia's vice-chairman, as she's the only one of us who has her own phone line with her own number. Without that, the club wouldn't work nearly as smoothly. That's why we meet in her room.

"What about Kid-Kits?" Kristy asked.

Kid-Kits are another of Kristy's great ideas. Each of us has a kit (made from a cardboard box) filled with hand-me-down toys, colouring books, crayons and whatever things we think the kids we sit for would enjoy. We don't bring them to every job, but they're always a hit when we do.

"We restocked most of the kits two weeks ago," I reported. "Anyone need any new stuff?" I looked around as everyone shook their heads, no.

"Is there anything else we're going to need money for?" Kristy asked the group.

"A refill pad of paper and a new notebook," Mary Anne said. "This record book is about full and so is our club notebook." Mary Anne is the club secretary. She's in charge of scheduling and is first-class at it. She keeps a record book filled with clients' names, addresses and phone numbers, rates paid, special details about the children we sit for, and all of *our* schedules – when I'm going to be in New York, when Jessi has a ballet class, when Mal has an orthodontist appointment, when Kristy has to coach her softball team. Everything. With this information, she schedules the babysitting jobs we take. The record book was Kristy's idea, but Mary Anne makes it work.

41

In the notebook we all record our baby-sitting experiences, sort of the way you write in a diary. Everybody reads it, so we all know what's happening to our clients.

I dug into the envelope and came up with a five-dollar note. "This should cover a pack of paper and a new notebook," I said, handing her the note.

"Anything else?" asked Kristy.

"I can't think of anything," said Shannon, who has taken over Dawn's job as alternate officer (at least until Dawn returns). Being alternate means she has to know how to do everyone's job in case someone's away ill.

"How much is left in the treasury?" Kristy asked me.

"Twenty," I said, "and I'm about to collect more." Everyone frowned and grumbled the way they always do when it's time to pay subs.

Kristy leaned forward. "We should have enough money to do it," she said thoughtfully.

"Do what?" asked Mal, who was sitting cross-legged on the floor.

"Cover the cost of having some leaflets photocopied. The other day Mary Anne told me that a lot of our regular clients are going on holiday in early July. I

42

thought this might be a good time to try to drum up some new customers. Claudia's drawing gave me the idea. We could put the sketch at the top, and writing underneath it. What do you think?" Kristy smiled, obviously very pleased with her idea.

"It's a great idea, but this might not be the best time to look for new business," I said sheepishly. I wasn't looking forward to telling Kristy I'd be going away. Being short-handed makes her very uneasy. But I had no choice. "I'm going on holiday the first two weeks in July. Claud's coming with me."

"What?" Kristy cried.

"Er, Kristy," Jessi spoke up from her spot next to Mal. "It's not a good time for Mal or me, either. We were about to ask you if you could spare us for the first two weeks of July."

"Why?" Kristy asked, looking very stressed.

Jessi and Mal exchanged anxious glances. "Jessi and I have been offered paid jobs as counsellors for the first two-week session of the day camp run by the Community Centre," Mal explained. "Mary Anne told us things were going to be slow, so we thought maybe we'd try it."

"Have you accepted the jobs yet?" Kristy asked.

"Sort of," Jessi admitted. "But a lot of the kids we usually sit for are signed up for the day camp, so it's almost like taking regular sitting jobs. I mean, if they're in camp, their parents won't be coming here."

Kristy folded her arms and sighed. "Logan's going away too, isn't he, Mary Anne?" Mary Anne nodded. "So that leaves Mary Anne, Shannon and me to cover all the jobs in early July. That's just great!"

"It really will be slow," Mary Anne said soothingly. "It's starting already. It's five-thirty-eight and the phone hasn't rung once. When was the last time *that* happened?" She was right. We'd usually arranged two or three jobs by now.

"OK," Kristy said, clearly still annoyed.

"I've got an idea," I offered, wanting to make Kristy feel better. "Why don't you lot all plan to come out to Fire Island for a four-day weekend over the Fourth of July?"

"We'll probably be working," said Mal.

"We hardly ever have jobs over the Fourth," Mary Anne said thoughtfully. "It's a real family holiday."

44

"I don't know," said Kristy. "I'd feel as though we were letting our customers down."

"I know!" cried Claudia, holding up her sketch. "We can make some leaflets, but instead of drumming up new clients we'll just write, 'The BSC will be off from July 3 to July 7, Happy Fourth!' That way our customers will have advance warning."

"Come on, Kristy," I said. "Live a little. Take a break."

Kristy frowned, but her eyes were thoughtful. "Maybe. I just don't know. Maybe."

4th CHAPTER

"We're on our way!" I cried out happily as the train pulled out of the Stoneybrook station. Claudia leaned across me and waved out of the window to her mother, who was still on the platform. She'd taken a break from her job and driven us to the station straight after school. Kristy and Shannon had come to say goodbye, too.

Soon they were out of sight. "This is so exciting," said Claudia, settling back in her seat. "I'm really glad Kristy agreed to come out on the Fourth with Mary Anne and Shannon. It's going to be great!" Suddenly Claudia frowned. "Gosh, I'm sorry. Here I'm going on about how happy I am and forgetting how bad you must feel about Robert. Was it hard to say goodbye to him at the end of school today?"

46

Of course, the true answer was, *Not at all. See you tomorrow,* was the exact text of the farewell speech I'd given to Robert.

"It wasn't too bad," I said (which was perfectly true).

"I suppose you'll really miss him," Claudia said.

"I'll be all right," I assured her.

"I really admire the mature way you're handling this," Claudia said.

"Thank you," I replied. So far, I hadn't actually lied to her, but I was starting to feel rather guilty anyway. Is allowing someone to continue thinking something which isn't true the same as lying? It felt uncomfortably close.

I pushed the guilty feelings aside. After all, I wasn't hurting anyone. "What's the first thing you want to do when we get there?" I asked Claudia.

"Head for the beach," she replied. Soon we were happily planning every second of our holiday.

The train journey to the city takes just under two hours. At last we pulled into Grand Central Station. "I love the city, but it scares me a bit," Claudia admitted as she pulled one of her two flowered bags down from the overhead luggage rack.

"You can't be half as scared as Dawn

was when we all came to the city together," I said. "Remember that?"

"She was pretty nervous," Claudia agreed. I laughed as I watched Claud struggle with her bags. "I hope the house Dad's rented has got big cupboards," I said. Claudia and I are too much alike when it comes to clothing. We'd both packed far more than we'd ever need! Like Claudia, I also had two suitcases, as well as two tennis rackets.

We wobbled off the train, staggering under the weight of all our stuff.

"Oh, my gosh!" Dad laughed when he saw us coming. He hurried towards us from the information desk, where he'd been waiting, and took our bags, leaving us the rackets.

We hailed a taxi and rode back to his flat. That night Dad ordered in some Middle Eastern food. We ate falafel sandwiches with pitta bread, babaghanouj (mashed aubergine with garlic and tahini) and stuffed vine leaves. I love this kind of food and you *can't* find it in Stoneybrook. (They make babaghanouj at Dawn's favourite health food restaurant, but it just doesn't taste as good, if you ask me.) Then Dad finished off some last-minute work on his computer, while Claudia and I watched a Johnny Depp film on cable

48

TV (Claud and I both think he's really gorgeous).

We went to bed early as we'd be getting up at six the next morning. Claud slept on the futon in my room. "You know," she said as I was just falling asleep, "I really appreciate your bringing me with you. I mean, you don't get to see your father that much, so it would have been understandable if you didn't want anybody else to come with you. But you wanted me to come too. I think that's really nice."

"Of course I wanted you to come," I said sleepily. "I think you'll like it there."

"You're a great friend, Stacey," Claudia said.

"So are you, Claud. Goodnight."

"Night."

My eyes were closed, but a small pang of guilt was keeping me from falling asleep. Claudia was right. This was a unique chance to spend time with my father. But what I was really *most* excited about was spending time with Robert. And would Claudia have thought I was such a great friend if she knew I hadn't told her about Robert being there?

I pushed these thoughts out of my mind. I wasn't hurting anyone, so I wasn't going to feel guilty. I turned on my side and went to sleep.

The next morning, Claudia, Dad and I ate breakfast at a nearby coffee shop. No one spoke much, as none of us is what you'd call a morning person. Then Dad hailed a taxi. He helped the driver load our luggage into the boot, and we rode down to Pennsylvania Station where you catch the Long Island Railroad trains.

Dad slept all the way out to Jamaica Station. There I had to shake him to wake him up. We all lugged our stuff across the platform, where we caught another train to Patchogue, which is out on Long Island. By the time we dragged our stuff off the train at the Patchogue station, we'd been travelling for more than two hours.

Dad put our bags in a taxi which was going to drive us to the ferry dock. "Davis Park, here we come," he said as we pulled into the large ferry car park in time to catch the next ferry over to Fire Island.

That's when it hit me. The ferry! Would Robert be on it already?

As we climbed out of the taxi, I scanned the dock area. It was easy to spot the *Kiki*, the ferry that would take us over. I looked at the dock around the boat and at the open upper deck. There was no sign of Robert. But what if he was inside? What

50

if we bumped into him? Dad didn't know what Robert looked like, but Claudia certainly did. What was I going to do?

"Come on, girls," said my father when the last of our gear was unloaded. I picked up one of my suitcases, still searching the area for any sign of Robert.

"Stacey, you seem so jumpy," said Claudia while Dad bought our tickets at the office by the dock.

"Oh, just the excitement of being on holiday, I suppose," I told her (another half truth). "Wait for me here, OK? I just have to run and see the boat. I can't wait another minute."

"I'll come too," said Claudia.

"No," I said, a bit too forcefully. "I mean, no, you stay here and tell Dad where I've gone. Please?"

"All right," Claudia said, looking puzzled.

I ran to the dock and up to a man wearing a heavy denim jacket and a black cap. "Is Robert Brewster working on this boat at the moment?" I asked anxiously.

The man jerked his head to the side thoughtfully. "Robert Brewster," he repeated as if he was trying to remember the name. Then his eyes lit up. "Oh, the new kid. No. He's not on this run. Wait a minute, maybe he *is* scheduled. Sorry,

51

but I'm not sure. Why don't you go on board and check."

"Thanks," I said, as I ran on to the ferry. I glanced quickly around the lower level with its long wooden benches. He wasn't there. I ran up the white metal steps to the top deck. No Robert.

I hurried back off the deck and got off the boat, almost running straight into Dad and Claudia. "I just *had* to see the boat," I panted.

"I've never seen you this excited about anything," Claudia commented.

"Why shouldn't I be?" I asked, taking a racket from her. I still wasn't positive Robert wasn't on the boat. Maybe I'd just missed him.

Together we walked on to the lower deck of the ferry. "Here's a good spot," said Dad, putting some bags down on a bench.

Claudia smiled. "It looks good to me."

The boat filled up quickly. Ten minutes later it pulled away from the dock.

"Let's take a walk around the ferry," suggested Claudia.

"Oh, no," I said quickly. "I . . . er . . . I get very seasick if I walk around on a moving boat. I'd better stay sitting." I did *not* want to run into Robert unexpectedly, just in case he was on board.

Claudia frowned quizzically. "Since when?"

"Oh, always. It's just with ferries this size."

My dad was reading *The New York Times*. He flipped the paper down and shot me a questioning look. Luckily, he decided to say nothing.

I unzipped one of my bags and pulled out a magazine. "There's a quiz in here I want to do," I said. "Test Your Boy Appeal."

"OK," Claudia agreed.

Remembering the quiz was like a stroke of genius because it took us most of the trip to complete it. By then, Claudia seemed to have lost the urge to roam.

When we got to the dock, we gathered up our things and joined the slow line of passengers disembarking. I was able to relax at last. We'd made the crossing without running into Robert. He probably wasn't on the boat at all.

As I stepped off the ferry, the first thing that struck me was the smell of the sea air. It was salty and fresh. We were just a ferry ride from Long Island but it was as if we'd landed in a very different seaside world.

A balding man in a peach-coloured aer-tex shirt and beige shorts met us at the dock. "This is my friend, Stu Majors," Dad introduced us. "He has a house here, and he's the one who arranged for us to rent his friend's house at such short notice."

"Thanks, Mr Majors," I said. "It's great to be here." I noticed that Mr Majors was pulling an empty red truck. You know – the kind kids have. For a second I thought he must be crazy. Then I saw that a lot of people had them. They were pulling their suitcases and gear in them.

That's when I noticed something even more unusual about Fire Island. There were no cars! Not one. Not even a road. Everyone was walking on narrow wooden boardwalks, pulling their red trucks behind them.

"Come on," said Mr Majors as he and Dad loaded our stuff into his truck. "I'll walk you to your house."

As we walked along the bay side, where we'd landed, there was nothing at all like a town, just wooden houses and low-growing shrubs and pine trees. "Look at the sign on that house," said Claudia. A sign hanging by the door read: Bedside Manor.

"A doctor rents that house," Mr Majors explained. "Get it?"

"Oh, bedside manner," I giggled. "Got it. What's our house called?"

"The Sandpiper."

"Pretty," I commented approvingly. The house *was* pretty, too. It was set half-way between the bay and the sea on the other side. You could see the sea from the big window in the kitchen. There were four cosy bedrooms.

"Let's sleep in this room together," said Claudia as we stepped into a room with twin beds.

"Don't you want your own room?" I asked.

"No, it will be more like a sleepover if we share a room," Claudia insisted.

"All right," I agreed.

We unpacked quickly, putting most of our things in the plain wooden chests of drawers and stuffing the rest in the narrow wardrobe. Then we decided to explore the island.

Dad and Mr Majors were sitting in the kitchen talking. "We're going out, Dad," I said.

"There's a pizza place in Watch Hill," said Mr Majors.

"Where's that?" asked Claudia eagerly. Mr Majors gave us directions, but I wasn't sure I could follow them.

"You'll find everything," Mr Majors

called as we went out of the door. "The community isn't that big."

As it turned out, I discovered what he meant sooner than I expected. We set off along the boardwalk, with Claudia keeping a sharp eye out for the landmarks Mr Majors had mentioned. We didn't find Watch Hill straight away, but we did come to a place called the Harbour Store. "I need a drink," Claudia decided.

While we waited inside to pay for her Coke, I realized we'd returned to the harbour area by way of a back walkway. The *Kiki* was in the dock. Passengers were streaming out of it. It had left the island and returned again.

Claudia paid for her drink, and she and I were just leaving when we bumped into someone coming in the front door of the store.

It was Robert!

5th CHAPTER

monday

Mal and I have real summer jobs! We'll get paycheques and everything! It's totally exciting. Our baby-sitting experience gives Mal and me a real advantage over the other junior counsellors. Still, taking care of a whole big bunch of kids at once is different from caring for a few at a time. And, sorry to say, our first day as counsellors did _not_ go smoothly.

57

Jessi and Mal arrived at the Stoneybrook Community Centre filled with excitement. They went straight to the office of Adele Lebeque, the head of the day camp programme. She made them fill in a few forms, and then she walked them down to the basketball court where the other counsellors had assembled.

The camp had already held an introductory day, which Mal and Jessi had attended. There they'd received the Stoneybrook Day Camp T-shirts which they had on that morning. They'd seen most of the other counsellors, too, but hadn't had much time to talk to them.

The older counsellors were in the fourteen-to-sixteen range. The junior counsellors were mostly twelve or thirteen. Jessi and Mal had got the jobs because they'd been so highly recommended by Mrs Braddock, a BSC client who's a friend of Miss Lebeque. They were the youngest junior counsellors.

"This is Laura Sanchez." Miss Lebeque introduced them to a tall, slim girl with large dark eyes and long, wavy, dark hair. "You two are in her team, with the eight- to nine-year-olds."

"Hi," Laura said with a smile. She pointed to a dark-skinned boy and a blonde girl standing a little way off. "Raj

58

and Amy over there will be working with us. We'll divide our kids into three sections. We'll all be doing things together, as a group, but you'll be responsible for the kids in your section. For now, I'm going to give you two the biggest sections. You can handle it together. OK?"

"OK!" said Mal with a smile. She was glad she and Jessi wouldn't be separated.

At nine-thirty, they went outside and met the two buses which were arriving loaded with day campers. "Tigers over here!" Laura shouted as the kids began milling about the car park. The campers had received their group assignments on the introductory day. The eight- to nine-year-olds were the Tigers.

The kids gathered around Laura. "Hey, Mal!" cried Vanessa Pike, Mal's nine-year-old sister. Vanessa looks a bit like Mal, with reddish brown hair, freckles and glasses. Next to Vanessa stood a girl with short blonde hair (with a trailing tail) and big brown eyes. She was Vanessa's best friend, Haley Braddock.

Jessi and Mal also spotted some other BSC clients looking for their groups. Jessi saw her younger sister, Becca. Three other Pike kids – Nicky, Margo and Claire – were there, too, together with Matt Braddock, Haley's younger brother.

59

"Vanessa, Haley," Jessi called as she beckoned to them. The girls joined Jessi and Mal. "Stay near us," Jessi told them. "Then maybe you'll be in our section."

As she'd said she would, Laura split the seventeen Tigers into three sections of five, five and seven. Jessi and Mal got the seven. Vanessa and Haley were two of them.

Checking a chart on her clipboard, Laura told the Tigers that they were scheduled to use the pool first. "Get changed, and we'll meet by the shallow end," she told them.

Jessi and Mal led their section into the community centre and down to the changing rooms. Then Raj went into the changing room with the boys, and Jessi, Mal and Amy went with the girls.

Some of the girls weren't shy, and changed right out in the open. Others held their swimsuits and waited for a cubicle to be free. Haley and Vanessa were among the ones who stood waiting for cubicles, their swimsuits rolled up in their towels.

At last two cubicles, side by side, opened up at the same time. Haley and Vanessa each went into one of them. "I'm so glad you're in my section," Haley said to Vanessa, tossing her T-shirt to the top of the cubicle as she changed.

60

"Me, too," Vanessa agreed, picking her shorts up off the floor as she stepped out of them. "This summer is going to be so much fun. Hey, wait till you see my new swimsuit. It's cool."

"I've got a new one, too," said Haley. "I can't wait to show you."

Haley and Vanessa came out of their cubicles, smiling. Instantly, their smiles faded. Vanessa's hands flew to her hips as the two girls stood staring at one another.

They had on the exact same swimsuit: it had red and white stripes, and a red ruffle along the neckline.

"I can't believe you went and got the same swimsuit!" Vanessa cried angrily. "After I told you I was getting it."

"You did not!" Haley cried.

"I showed it to you in the catalogue!" Vanessa shouted, her voice growing higher. "I said, 'My mum is getting me this swimsuit.'"

"You said you couldn't decide between the red stripes and the purple checks and you thought you liked the purple checks better," Haley disagreed.

"I did not!" Vanessa fumed. "I said I couldn't decide but I liked the red stripes."

"You did not," Haley insisted.

61

"What are you saying? That I'm lying?" Vanessa asked angrily.

Haley folded her arms. "You must be, because you did *not* say you were getting the red stripes."

"I did!" Vanessa yelled.

By that time, most of the other girls had gone out to the pool area. Amy had gone with them. "Come on," said Jessi. "We have to go outside."

"I'm not going out there!" cried Vanessa. "We look stupid in the same swimsuits!"

"Just tell everybody you're best friends, and you chose matching swimsuits," Mal suggested.

"*Ex*-best friends." Vanessa sulked.

Haley's eyes widened when Vanessa said that. "If that's how you want to be about it, that's fine with me!" she shouted and stomped out of the changing rooms.

"Come on, Vanessa," said Mal. "We've got to go."

"Mal, she went out there first. Now it will look like I'm copying her instead of her copying me. But she did copy me." Vanessa wailed. "I can't go out there in the same swimsuit. I'll feel like a real idiot!"

"I'll swap swimsuits with you," Jessie suggested.

62

They tried swapping swimsuits, but Jessi's was too big on Vanessa and Vanessa's was too tight on Jessi. "Come on, you two," Laura called into the changing rooms.

"Vanessa, just put on your swimsuit and come out," Mal said, growing impatient. "It won't be that bad."

"Oh, all right," Vanessa sulked. "But I can't believe that out of all the zillion suits in the world, Haley had to go out and buy the one she *knew* I was going to get. She did it on purpose, too."

"I'm sure she didn't," Mal said. "Why would she do that?"

"Because once I showed her the swimsuit, she wanted it and she didn't care how I would feel if she got the same one. She can be like that – selfish!"

"I don't think Haley's like that," Jessi disagreed.

"Well why else would she do something like this?" Vanessa argued.

Jessi and Mal didn't know what to say. They didn't know why Haley would buy the same swimsuit.

With her head down, Vanessa trudged out to the pool area.

"Jessi, Mal, you can't leave your group for so long," Laura said as they followed Vanessa towards the shallow end.

63

"Sorry," said Jessi. "We had a bit of a problem."

"Is the problem solved?" Laura asked.

"We think so," said Mal.

"Good work then." Laura smiled. "Next time, just split up if you have to." Laura blew her whistle, and all the kids looked at her. She told them they were going to get into two teams for a game of water volleyball.

"I'm not going to be in her team," Vanessa said immediately, glaring at Haley.

"All right, then split up," Mallory said crossly. She helped Raj and Amy divide the Tigers up, eight on one side and seven on the other, while Jessi and Laura hooked up a long net across the shallow area of the pool.

"Hey, those two should be in the same team because they're wearing the same swimsuit!" shouted a heavy-set boy with blond spikey hair. Haley and Vanessa stared daggers at each other.

Laura's rule was that the kids could only hit the big beach ball with their heads. As the ball was so light, it didn't hurt. Soon the kids were laughing hysterically – all but Haley and Vanessa. Their two stony faces matched as perfectly as their suits.

64

When it was Vanessa's turn to serve the ball, she slammed it in Haley's direction with so much force it looked as though she was trying to knock her out. Light as the ball was, Haley wanted to knock it out of her way quickly. And she did – she moved so fast that she slipped and went under water.

She came up spluttering. "Vanessa did that on purpose!" she shouted.

"Not so hard," Laura said to Vanessa.

Vanessa just smiled as Haley pushed her wet fringe out of her eyes.

To Jessi, it seemed as though the hour in the pool went on for ever. But at last it was time for arts and crafts in the art room. "Well, at least they can't try to drown one another in there," Jessi whispered to Mal as they herded the kids inside.

"I'm going to show you all how to make lanyards today," Laura was saying. She put some big spools of different coloured plastic cord on the table. She also put out a cardboard box of tin whistles to put on the ends of the braided cords when they were ready. "Ask a counsellor to help you cut four strands each in whatever colours you want," Laura instructed the kids. "They should all be about three metres long. When everybody's

65

ready, I'll show you how to braid them together."

Jessi, Mal, Laura, Amy and Raj helped the kids measure and cut their cords. There was a lot of careful consideration – the kids chose their colours as if it were a major decision.

While Mal was helping a petite girl called Alexis to choose between purple and red, Jessi helped Haley measure a blue piece. "I'd like to combine it with white, but *she's* got the white," said Haley. Jessi looked up and saw that *she* was Vanessa.

Vanessa heard Haley, but she spoke to Jessi. "Please tell *her* that it was bad enough that she copied my swimsuit. She can't have the same colour lanyard as I do, too."

"Would you inform her that my lanyard will be white and blue, *not* white and red like the ugly one she's making. And she does not own the colour white," Haley shot back. "Just like she doesn't own the rights to every swimsuit she happens to see in a catalogue."

"Jessi, tell her that only a real peabrain can't choose her own stuff and has to copy someone else's every move," said Vanessa. "I think I'll keep the white cord for now so *someone* won't be able to copy

66

me by making her lanyard white and another colour."

"That's enough, you two," said Jessi. "Why don't you just stop this and be friends again?"

"Never!" said Haley, crossing her arms.

"Ever," agreed Vanessa.

Jessi sighed. If this kept up, it was going to be a long two weeks!

6th CHAPTER

Saturday

Dear Mary Anne,

Greetings from Ocean Ridge, Fire Island. Ocean Ridge is right next to Davis Park (in case you were confused). I can't wait until you, Shannon and Kristy get here. You will LOVE it !!!!!! Everything is great. See you soon. Can't wait!!!

Love, Stacey

When I told Claudia I'd known Robert would be at Davis Park all along, she was pretty cross. She went stamping out of the Harbour Store and I had to chase her down the boardwalk. "I can't believe you've been lying to me!" she grumbled when I eventually caught up with her.

"I didn't think you'd come if you knew about Robert," I admitted. "I didn't tell you because I really wanted you to come."

The frown stayed on Claudia's face, but her dark eyes softened a bit. "Really?"

"Yes!" I insisted. "Robert will be working all day almost every day."

"Why did you lie?" Claudia asked poutily.

"I've just told you!" I cried.

"Aren't we best friends?" said Claudia.

"Of course we are."

"Best friends don't lie and keep secrets. I don't really mind that Robert's here. That's OK. In fact, it's rather romantic. But it bugs me that you lied."

I put my hand on her arm. "You're right. I'm sorry. Would you have come if I'd told you about Robert?"

A small smile formed on Claudia's lips. "No."

"See?" I cried.

Claudia laughed a little. "You should have told me anyway."

69

"Then you wouldn't have come!"

The problem wasn't exactly resolved, but I was glad Claudia wasn't angry any more. She sighed and shook her head. "I suppose it's nice that you wanted me here that badly."

"I did. And I won't lie to you ever again."

"Promise?"

"Promise," I said. "But, listen, Dad doesn't know about Robert, so don't mention his being here. OK?"

"You shouldn't lie to your father either," Claudia said.

I raised my eyebrows. "You can't talk! You hide junk food and sneak out your Nancy Drew books at night!"

Claudia sighed. "I suppose you're right. All right. I won't say anything."

Just then I saw Robert coming down the boardwalk towards us. That's one of the things I love about him. He always backs me up. Another guy would have just taken off, not wanting any part of the problem. Not Robert. After giving me a little space, he was coming to see if he could help make things right.

"Hi, Claudia," he said, flashing his great smile. There was laughter in his eyes, which made the whole situation seem more funny than terrible.

70

"Hello, Robert," said Claudia, smiling. Right then, I knew everything was going to be all right. The three of us went to the ice-cream stand near the dock. Robert and Claudia got cones. I was stuck with a cup of soda water, but I didn't care. I was glad everyone was friends. What could be better than sitting outside on a crystal blue day in a gorgeous, beachy place with my two favourite people? Nothing!

For the next few days, everything was perfect. I couldn't believe how relaxed Dad was. He was like a different person. For one thing, he did *not* bring work with him. (All right. He had a few reports with him, which he read on the beach. But for my dad, that's *nothing*.) Apart from that, he was pretty much letting Claudia and me come and go as we pleased. "This isn't New York," he said. "You're very safe here. The only way in or out is the ferry. I don't even have to worry about you being hit by a car."

His relaxed attitude made everything so simple. On Sunday morning, before either Claudia or Dad was even up, I got out of bed and met Robert on the corner of the boardwalk. I walked him down to the dock so he could be on the first ferry over to Patchogue.

What a great way to start the day! I did it again on Monday and Tuesday. Robert would put his arm around my shoulder and we'd walk along with the gulls swooping overhead. Not many people were up yet. It was as if we were in our own private place. We wouldn't talk much. But I felt so close to Robert, closer than ever before. It was as if I could feel the light touch of his hand on my shoulder for the rest of the day.

Each day, by the time I got back, Dad was up brewing a pot of coffee. He and I would sit and have breakfast together. We'd usually be practically finished by the time a sleepy-eyed Claudia would stumble in. "Sorry I slept so late," she said the first day, Sunday.

"Do whatever you like," said Dad. "You're on holiday."

Well, hello Mr Mellow!

That's what we all did – just what we liked. On Sunday morning, Dad came to the beach with us. On Monday morning, Mr Majors invited us to use his private tennis backboard. That was fun, but we only went once. It was as if a sort of holiday slowness was settling over us.

Dad was a bit busier. He played chess with Mr Majors on Monday afternoon, and he went over there on Tuesday, too.

In fact, he spent a lot of time at Mr Majors' house. I'd never heard of Mr Majors before, so I was rather surprised that they were such good friends. Maybe Dad just needed some adult company.

Claudia and I spent most of Monday and Tuesday down by the sea. We'd swim, ride the waves and collect shells. Claudia built dozens of elaborate sand castles. (You haven't seen a sand castle till you've seen a Claudia Kishi castle!) They were absolutely gorgeous, with towers, tunnels, turrets, drawbridges made of driftwood, and windows made of coloured beach glass. Once she even sand-sculpted an advancing dragon, complete with seaweed spikes along his back.

I couldn't believe that Claudia didn't mind the way the sea would wash these creations away, but she didn't. In fact, Claud found a way to turn their destruction into art. She started bringing her camera to the beach, and photographing the waves' work. She'd get completely covered with sand as she lay on her stomach with her camera in front of her. She'd shoot the water rushing into her moat, the surf crashing up and tumbling down one of her carefully made sand walls. She'd photograph the orange-pink sunset on her half-crashed castle. The different stages of the castles' destruction were as interesting to her as their creation.

With Claudia busy making her castles, and Dad spending so much time over at Mr Majors' place, it wasn't difficult for me to get away to see Robert. I ran down to the dock whenever I knew the ferry would be getting in. Robert usually had about half an hour before he had to go out again on another run.

On the days Claudia and I were alone, I just left Claud on the beach when I went to the dock. On Sunday, when Dad was there, I had to bring her with me, or Dad would have suspected something. Then it was a bit awkward. I told Claudia she should stay with us, but she knew we wanted to be alone.

She was great, though. "I'll go and browse in the Harbour Store," she'd say. (Not that there's all that much to see there. It's mostly groceries and toiletries.)

Going out at night was tougher on Claudia. She had to come out with me or Dad would have thought something was strange. But, if she wanted to give Robert and me time alone, there really wasn't anywhere for her to go by herself.

Luckily, on Sunday, we found the pizzeria on Watch Hill. The three of us

74

went there for pizzas. When Robert and I got up to leave, Claudia stayed seated. "I'm going to stay here and read my book," she said. She'd brought along a book on photography.

"Are you sure?" I asked.

"Yes, I'd really like to read this," she insisted. I knew she was just trying to give Robert and me space.

"All right," I said. "We're just going to have a walk on the beach." My moonlit walks with Robert were so romantic. That first week, a big full moon was coming in. It outlined the crashing waves in silver light. We'd walk along, and Robert would tell me funny or interesting things that had happened on the ferry that day. (For instance, one afternoon a pet chinchilla had escaped from its carrying case. The ferry ride turned into a mad chinchilla hunt, as the animal scurried around below the seats.)

'This is turning into the best summer ever," Robert said, that first night. "A great job during the day, and the chance to see you every free minute I have."

"It's great for me, too," I said happily. "Things have worked out so perfectly."

Gently, Robert kissed me, there in the moonlight. It was like something out of a wonderful dream.

75

I made it back to the pizzeria just as it was closing. Claudia was waiting for me outside. "Sorry," I said. "I didn't know they closed so early."

"That's OK," said Claudia. She really didn't seem to mind my going off with Robert.

When we got home, Dad was out. I didn't even hear him come in. The next day, Dad told us he'd be going over to Mr Majors' house in the evening. Claudia and I left after supper together, but she went back home half an hour later. When I came in an hour or so after that, Dad was still out.

On Tuesday night, Dad left before we did. "I'll just stay at home tonight," Claudia volunteered. "Your dad probably won't come in till late again."

"Are you sure you won't be bored?" I asked her.

"It's OK," she replied with a shrug. "Being a little bored won't kill me."

7th CHAPTER

Wednesday

Hi Char—

Told you I'd send a postcard. Who is baby-sitting for you while I'm on vacation? Have you seen Kristy, Shannon, or Mary Anne? Jessi wrote and said Vanessa and Haley are fighting. How is that affecting you? It must be hard having your two buds at war. I hope they make peace soon. Things here are great. The time is going way too fast. The Fourth of July should be wonderful. See you soon.

Love, Stacey

77

The time did seem to be zooming by. They say that time flies when you're having fun. I think it's true.

On Wednesday, as we made our way down to the dock to meet the noon ferry, Claudia spotted a poster pinned to a tree. (Claudia was with me because Dad had come down to the beach with us that morning, and I didn't want him wondering where I was off to, alone.) Claudia stopped and read the poster aloud. It said: *Join the Fourth of July Fun! March in our annual parade. Come in costume. Make a float.*

"July the first! That's today!" Claudia cried.

"So?" I questioned.

"So, we have to be in this parade," said Claudia. "There's absolutely *nothing* to do around here. But this is something! We can't let it go by."

"You said you weren't bored," I reminded her.

"I said it wouldn't kill me to be bored," she corrected me. "It won't kill me but I'm not crazy about it."

"You mean you're not having a good time?" I asked, suddenly feeling rather guilty about being with Robert so much.

"I wouldn't say that exactly," Claudia replied. "But it isn't quite the way I

78

pictured it. I thought I was going to spend time with *you*."

I pretended to brush my hair away from my face, but I was really sneaking a look at my watch. The ferry was pulling in *now*. Part of me wanted to rush Claudia along to meet it, but another part knew this wasn't the right moment to do that.

"We *are* spending time together," I said. "Like this morning."

"But it feels as if you're just killing time with me till you can see Robert again. And that's not a great feeling."

For the first time, I put myself in Claudia's shoes. (Sandals, I suppose.) Suddenly I could understand how she felt. "I'm just trying to spend time with you *and* Dad *and* Robert. I don't want you to feel bad, because I'm so glad you're here. Why don't you have lunch with us on the dock today?"

"I don't think so," said Claudia. "I'd just be in the way."

"No, you wouldn't," I insisted. Of course, I loved having lunch alone with Robert. But that wasn't more important than Claudia's feelings.

I was relieved when Claudia started walking again. "I *would* be in the way. Besides, I want to go to the Harbour Store and sign up for this parade. All I want is for you to promise to march in it. I'm going to make costumes and everything."

I didn't exactly love the idea of parading around the boardwalks in a costume, but how could I say no? "OK," I agreed, praying that Robert would be out on the ferry and wouldn't see me that day. "And, listen, I'll tell Robert I can't see him tonight."

"You don't have to do that," said Claudia.

I felt another little twinge of guilt. The truth was that one of the other crew members was ill and Robert was working the late runs for him. He wouldn't be free till ten o'clock, anyway. "I don't mind," I said.

Claudia smiled. "All right, if you really don't mind."

When we got to the dock, Robert was waiting with a paper bag of food for our picnic. "Everything OK?" he asked.

"Fine," I said.

"I bought some lunch while I was waiting," Robert said, nodding towards the bag he was holding. "I thought you'd be here soon."

"We just stopped to read about the parade on the Fourth," Claudia explained.

"That should be fun," he said. "Too

bad I won't get to see it. I'll be in the middle of the bay when it starts."

Good thing, I thought, relieved.

Claudia dug into the pocket of her denim shorts and pulled out three rolls of film. "Is there any place to get film developed on the other side?" she asked Robert.

"There's a one-hour place nearby," he replied. "I could ask one of the guys who live in Patchogue to drop it off for you."

Claudia handed him the film and fished a crumpled twenty-dollar note out of her pocket. "I don't really need it in an hour, but I do want it soon."

"No problem," said Robert, taking the money from her.

Claudia went off, and Robert and I found a grassy spot not far from the dock. "Good news," Robert told me as we unwrapped our sandwiches. "I don't have to work tonight. The guy I was covering for is feeling better."

"Oh, no!" I wailed. "I told Claudia I'd definitely do something with her tonight."

Robert looked disappointed. "Well, OK. That's all right. I'll find something to do." But I knew Robert didn't feel like sticking around the house where he was living. The couple he was staying with didn't have any kids, and he felt as though

81

he was a bit in their way. He couldn't wait for his family to arrive, so he could go and live with them and feel at home.

As we finished our lunch, I could see people beginning to gather around the ferry. That was a sure sign that it was almost time for the next run. "I'll miss you tonight," said Robert as he started stuffing paper napkins and wrappers back into the bag.

"Me, too," I said, wiping crumbs from my mouth. "But I'll see you after the next ferry."

"Maybe you should just spend the time with Claudia today," Robert suggested. (He's *so* sensitive!)

I probably should have, but I couldn't bear the thought of not seeing Robert till the following day. "It's all right," I said, brushing sand from the back of my shorts. "I'll spend tonight with her and she'll be OK."

Robert kissed me and went back to the ferry. I walked up to the Harbour Store, but Claudia wasn't there. I was just trying to decide where to look next when I saw her come out from one of the side walkways. She was all smiles. "Look what I found," she said, holding out a card as she ran to meet me.

I took the card from her and looked at

82

it. It was a drawing of a sand castle with fairy tale characters around it. There was a princess, her lady-in-waiting, a prince, a dragon and a court jester. The drawing appeared to be very old-fashioned, as if it were an illustration from an old storybook.

"I went for a walk and found this house painted pink," Claudia explained. "I stopped to look at it and noticed a sign outside saying 'Beach Glass Gallery, browsers welcome', so I went in. It's the loveliest little art gallery. I found this card in a box of antique cards for sale."

"It's pretty," I commented.

"It is. It also gave me a great idea for our parade costumes. We're going to be these characters, and we can make a sand castle float."

"Shouldn't you do something patriotic for the Fourth?" I questioned.

"No, no," Claudia said, waving her hand. "Everyone will be doing that. This is something beachy. That fits, too, don't you think so?"

"I suppose so," I agreed. "How will you make the float?"

"I haven't worked that out yet, but I will," Claudia said. From the thoughtful expression on her face, I could tell she was already at work on the project.

When we got back to the beach, Dad was gone. All our things were still on the blanket, though. Fire Island is the kind of place where you feel pretty safe leaving your things lying around. Claudia picked up her sketch pad and immediately began sketching the figures from the postcard. "I haven't got the right stuff to make all these costumes," she said, half to me, half to herself. "I bet we could send a fax to Kristy. Watson's got a fax machine in his office, hasn't he?"

"Yes, he has. I think I've got his fax number in my address book."

"Good," said Claudia. "We can tell the others to bring costume stuff. I can write a note and give it to Robert, to fax on Long Island. Or maybe I'll take the ferry across myself and get the taxi into town."

"I'll come with you," I offered.

"That would be great," Claudia said, smiling as she continued to sketch.

Claudia was so intent on her costume sketches that I didn't feel guilty about meeting Robert twice more. Then we went back to the house. There was a note from dad saying that he'd gone out to dinner with Mr Majors. "He really seems to like Mr Majors," said Claudia, tossing her sketchbook on to the kitchen worktop.

84

"I know," I agreed as I stood with the screen door open, brushing sand off my legs on to the porch. "He's always over there." I shook out my towel and draped it on the rail of the wooden deck outside. "Are you coming for pizzas again?"

"You bet!" Claudia said. "And I'm starving. Let's shower and go."

The house had two bathrooms, so we were able to shower at the same time. I pulled on a pair of green leggings and a sleeveless denim top. Claudia put on a pair of wild tie-dyed leggings and an over-sized T-shirt she'd designed and silk-screened herself. She'd painted a flock of birds flying diagonally across it.

We went to Watch Hill for pizzas, and who just happened to be sitting there? Robert. Was that my fault? No. We couldn't be rude, so we asked him to join us. Claudia didn't seem to mind. She chattered happily about her plans for our float. She'd come up with the idea of tying together four or five red trucks and laying a board across their tops. That would give her a flat surface to build a giant sand castle on.

"Sounds cool," said Robert. "If you want help with anything, let me know."

"I will," said Claudia. When we'd finished eating, Claudia got up to leave.

I wanted to linger with Robert for a while longer, but I didn't think I should.

Without even giving me time to say goodbye to him, Claudia headed for the door. I hurried after her. "Wait for me," I called as she continued to walk away.

"Go back inside with Robert," she grumbled, not stopping.

"Claudia! I didn't tell him to be there. Is that what you think?"

Claudia stopped and threw her arms in the air. "I don't know. Did you?"

"No!"

"This is crazy, Stacey. I wanted to spend some time with *you*, remember?"

"I know. And I didn't know he'd be there. But what's so bad about the three of us hanging around together? You were having a good time in there," I argued.

"I wasn't going to be rude to Robert. He's a nice guy. But that's not the point," said Claudia. "I thought we were going to spend this evening together."

"We will, starting from now."

Claudia shook her head and started walking again. "It's no good now. I know you'd rather not leave Robert. And he was looking at you with those big eyes like, *Please don't leave me*."

"He was not!"

86

"We'll just run into him wherever we decide to go."

Just then, Robert came out of the pizzeria. He didn't seem to know whether to come and join us or walk in the other direction. Then I had a great idea. "Claudia, I know what we can do. We'll have a nice dinner tomorrow night at the real restaurant, at the Casino. I'll tell Robert not to be there, so we'll be sure we won't be interrupted. OK?"

"OK," Claudia said, a smile washing away her frown. "It's a best friend date. Tomorrow, just you and me."

8th CHAPTER

Thursday

Hi, Mom!

Greetings from Fire Island. Everything here is great! The weather has been perfect. The house is gorgeous. Cloud and I are having a terrific time. Kristy, Shannon and Mary Anne arrive this weekend. We're all going to march in a Fourth of July parade. It should be silly but fun. I miss you.

Love, Stacey

Thursday was yet another super-beautiful day. In the morning, Claudia and I took the first ferry over to Patchogue. We took a taxi into town, and Claudia found a fax place. She sent a message to Watson's fax number telling Kristy, Shannon and Mary Anne to bring costume stuff. She even faxed a second page with her costume sketches on it.

On the way back, Robert had a break and sat with us. We left Claudia sketching on the lower deck and went up to the top deck together. A guy in an official ferry windbreaker with the name "Mitch" stitched on it came over to us. "Is this the amazing Stacey I've heard so much about?" he asked.

Robert nodded proudly. "The very same."

"This guy is crazy about you," Mitch teased. "Now I see why."

"Thanks," I said. "Nice to meet you."

When Mitch left I kissed Robert lightly on the cheek. I knew he liked me, but "crazy about" me? It sounded wonderful.

After we got off the ferry, Claudia and I hurried over to the beach. Dad was already there, reading a novel. Claudia started building small sand castles. She built five little ones in an hour. Some were tall and thin with high towers, others were

89

more ranch-style castles, low to the ground with sprawling courtyards. She said she was experimenting, trying to find a model that wouldn't crumble easily when she built a large-scale version for her parade float.

She was so engrossed in her castles that I didn't feel bad leaving her to go and meet the ferry. (Dad had already taken off, for more chess, or something.) I was there in time to see the boat pull into the dock. Robert spotted me from the upper deck and waved. I waved back. (It was so romantic. I thought about long ago days, and sailors coming home from the sea. I imagined myself as Robert's true love, waiting on the dock to greet him. I could easily picture myself in a long white skirt, with ribbons in my hair.)

As usual, I watched all the passengers stream off the boat, and then Robert appeared. "Wait till you hear this," he said, putting his arm around me. "A guy I work with – Mitch, the one you met this morning – he has this great sailing boat. He's taking it out for a sunset sail this evening and he's invited us to come along."

"Oh, that sounds so—" I was going to say wonderful, but I stopped myself. "I can't go."

90

"Why not?" he asked.

"Remember? I told you I'm going out with Claudia tonight."

"I forgot. Go out with her tomorrow night," Robert suggested.

"I can't. Tomorrow night Mary Anne, Shannon and Kristy will be here. Claudia really wants to do something together, just the two of us."

"Then do it after they leave," said Robert.

Robert was making sense. There was no reason why Claudia and I couldn't go to the Casino any night next week. But the idea of cancelling my arrangement with Claudia tonight didn't make me feel good. I had a strong feeling that Claudia wouldn't take it well. "Is this guy going to take his boat out any other evening?" I asked hopefully.

Robert shook his head. "He's lending it to a friend for the rest of July."

Angrily, I kicked a pebble with my trainer. "I'd really like to go. Maybe Claudia would understand. By tomorrow she'll have a whole house full of friends to do things with."

"You could ask her," said Robert.

"I can't," I muttered. "I just can't."

"OK. I'll tell Mitch we can't make it." Robert said, jamming his hands into his jeans pockets. I could tell he was disappointed. So was I.

"Wait," I said. I'd just had a brilliant thought. "The sun doesn't set till almost nine o'clock, right? What time is Mitch sailing?"

"He said to be down at the harbour no later than eight-thirty," Robert replied.

"If I have supper with Claudia at six, I can definitely be here by eight-thirty."

"Do you think so?"

"I don't see why not," I said. "It doesn't take more than two hours to eat supper. And at six o'clock, the restaurant shouldn't be crowded."

Robert's face relaxed into a smile. "That would work out great."

"I'll have to ask Dad, but I'm sure he'll say yes." I gave Robert a quick squeeze. "A sunset sail with you is too special to pass up."

I was walking on air for the rest of the day. What could be more romantic than a sunset sail? I kept picturing Robert kissing me as golden light bathed us in its glow, and the pure white sails billowed behind us. (Somehow, in my fantasy, I had on that flowing white dress again. And Mitch was *not* on board. Neither was anyone else. It was just Robert and me.)

At five o'clock, I didn't go and meet

92

the ferry. I wanted to get Claudia home so we could be at the Casino by six. "I'm not really hungry yet," Claudia protested as I hurriedly gathered up our towels and beach chairs.

"I'm starving. And you'll be hungry by six," I insisted.

"But we never eat that early."

"This is the beginning of the big Fourth of July weekend," I said. "You should have seen the last ferry to come in. It was *loaded* with people. If we don't turn up early we might not get seats at all."

"It's only Thursday," said Claudia, taking a folded beach chair from me.

"Robert says the weekends start on Thursday here. And the Fourth of July is a really busy weekend."

Claudia shrugged. "If you say so." Carrying most of the stuff myself (there was no time to hand things to Claudia), I led the way back to the house. It was five-fifteen when we walked in.

Dad was talking to someone on the phone. "OK, someone's just come in. Talk to you later," he said, ringing off quickly. For some reason he was wearing a guilty expression, as if we'd caught him doing something he shouldn't be doing.

"Who was that?" I asked suspiciously.

"Stu," Dad said.

93

I studied him. What could he and Stu be discussing that would make Dad look so guilty? I didn't have time to worry about it right then.

"Are you girls still planning to go out to dinner?" he asked.

Claudia nodded and sat down at the kitchen table. I took her arm and lifted her back up. "Come on, we have to get ready to go. We need to be there by six."

"Gosh! You're getting as punctuality-crazy as Kristy. Why do we have to be on time? We're on holiday. It isn't as though anyone's waiting for us," Claudia protested.

"I just don't want to stand around waiting for a table," I said.

"Calm down, will you?" Claudia mumbled. But at last she went to our shared room. She opened the wardrobe and stared at her clothes – just stared at them!

"What are you doing?" I asked, trying hard to sound relaxed. (And not succeeding.)

"Choosing something to wear," she answered. "I brought all this great stuff, and all I've worn since we landed is my swimsuit, T-shirts and shorts."

Sometimes Claudia can choose a great

94

outfit in seconds, so I decided not to worry about her being ready on time. I dashed through my shower. As I'd spent all day thinking about what I would wear, I knew exactly what to put on: this white and blue sundress with a dropped waist and a square sailor collar. It wasn't exactly the dress of my fantasy, but it was as close as I could get.

I ran into the bathroom to do my make-up, as the light in there was better. This evening, I decided I looked fine without make-up. Even with the factor fifteen sun block I usually wore, I'd got a light golden tan. I love the way I look with a tan. It makes my eyes bluer and gives me a wonderful glow. My hair was a little blonder from the sun, too. All I needed was a touch of lipstick.

"Ready?" I asked as I hurried back into the bedroom.

I took a deep breath in an effort to stay calm. Claudia was *still* staring into the wardrobe. I pulled a yellow sundress of mine off the rail and handed it to her. "Wear this. You'll look great in it."

Claudia held the dress out and studied it. "Do you really think so? I'm not sure yellow is a good colour for me."

"Claudia!" I cried. "What's the big deal? We don't even know anyone who will be at the restaurant. What do you even care?"

"Excuse me if I like looking nice," Claudia said, clearly miffed. She put my yellow dress back in the wardrobe and took out a blue denim pinafore dress. "I'll wear this."

Action at last! But it was all in slow motion. Claudia buttoned every button slowly. She smoothed away the packing wrinkles left in the dress one by one. Watching her brush her long hair nearly drove me insane. She began each brush stroke at the crown of her hair and then – ever so slowly – drew the brush down, down, down to the end. And then she would start all over again.

Eventually I couldn't stand it another second. I took the brush out of her hand. "You look gorgeous. Let's go."

"I've never seen this side of you, Stacey," Claudia said as I drew her out of the room, holding her wrist.

"What side?" I asked.

"I never knew you acted so crazy when you're hungry. Is it because of your diabetes?"

"Yes!" I said. "That's it! When I'm really hungry I act like this. I usually don't get this hungry at home but here I'm all off schedule." That, of course, was a

96

complete lie. But maybe if Claudia thought I needed food she'd move a bit faster.

Claudia went into the kitchen and opened the fridge. "*What* are you doing now?" I asked.

"I'm looking for something for you to eat," she said. "I think you should eat a snack before we go."

I shut the fridge. "No, come on, let's just sit down and have a nice supper that I can really enjoy. OK?"

"OK," she said.

Dad came into the kitchen. "You girls look lovely. If you need me tonight, call Stu Majors. He's having a party, so I might not be near the phone, but he'll find me and I'll call you right back if—"

"We won't need you, Dad," I said, pulling open the kitchen door. "'Bye."

"Have fun," he called after us as we hurried down the steps and on to the boardwalk. I waved back to him without even turning round.

"Slow down," Claudia complained. "I can't keep up with you."

Reluctantly, I slowed down a bit. I checked my watch. Six-fifteen – I was already fifteen minutes behind schedule.

It was six-twenty when we reached the

97

Casino. It was pretty empty. "I can't see any holiday crowds," Claudia pointed out.

"It's a good thing we're here early," I replied as we walked inside. The hostess came right over and seated us. Claudia asked for a table by the window. The hostess found us one, and handed us menus. I decided on flounder in a lemon sauce and put down my menu.

But Claudia kept reading, and reading, and reading. I began munching on a breadstick from the bread basket on the table. By that time I really did need to eat something. "What's the problem?" I asked her, several minutes later.

"Well, I can't decide between shrimp cocktail or crab's legs for a starter."

"You're having a starter?" I squeaked.

"Don't worry," said Claudia. "I've got enough cash. Order whatever you want. My parents gave me some money to take you out for a treat of some kind. Besides, I really do think you need to eat something straight away. Why don't you have the crab's legs and I'll have the shrimp and we'll share."

"All right," I agreed, just to get it over with. "It's nice of you to treat me. Now put down your menu so they know we're ready to order."

Instead, Claudia lifted her menu up again. "Just give me a minute. I can't decide between the lobster bisque and the clam chowder."

She was having soup too! "I thought you weren't hungry," I reminded her.

"I know," she laughed. "But everything looks so good."

Choosing her main course was another drawn-out decision for Claudia. By the time the waitress took our order my watch said it was five to seven. 'You have to allow twenty minutes for your lobster thermidor to be prepared," the waitress told Claudia.

"Why?" I asked sharply.

She explained that they started with a fresh lobster, boiled it and then cooked the meat with all the other ingredients before putting it back into the lobster shell. "Maybe you'd like something else," I said, although I hated the idea of beginning the decision-making all over again.

"No," Claudia said. "I'm in no rush."

Exactly. I, on the other hand, was in a huge rush. I couldn't tell Claudia that, though. The way I'd pictured it, Claudia and I would have a fun dinner and then stroll back to the house. Claudia would probably want to work on her parade project, and I'd just say I was going out for a while. She'd be happy because we'd spent time together. And I'd be happy because she was happy, and Robert and I could still have our romantic sail together.

Although it had sounded perfect, it wasn't turning out that way. By seven-thirty we'd eaten our starters and soup. (I was already full, and could have done without the main course altogether.) When Claudia's lobster thermidor arrived, she inhaled the warm scent of the creamy sauce with herbs and hunks of sauteed lobster meat floating in it. She savoured every bite, slowly. "This is heaven," she sighed.

JUST EAT!!!!! I wanted to scream. Of course, I couldn't. I just sat there choking down my fish. Even though it was delicious, I was too full and rushed to enjoy it.

By eight o'clock a waitress was clearing our table and wiping away the crumbs. I was craning my neck, looking for our own waitress so that I could signal for the cheque, when I heard Claudia ask a passing waiter: "Could you bring us a dessert menu?"

"Claudia, how could you eat dessert after all that?" I cried.

"I don't know." Claudia smiled. "Somehow I always have room for dessert. I bet they've got fresh fruit or something else you could eat."

"I couldn't eat another bite," I told her.

By eight-fifteen Claudia had finished her ice-cream sundae. My prediction about the Casino getting busy had also come true by then. While we'd been eating, the place had filled up. Our waitress was incredibly busy taking orders, delivering them, and *not* bringing us our cheque. By eight-twenty I stood up to get her attention.

She brought the cheque, and Claudia put down her money. It was eight-twenty-five before the waitress came back with the change.

"Let's go," I said to Claudia at last.

I'd estimated that I needed fifteen minutes to walk down to the dock. Ten minutes if I hurried. Five minutes if I ran like the wind.

I now had five minutes.

As we were hurrying along the boardwalk, Claudia pointed ahead. "Isn't that Robert?" she said. She was right! Robert was riding a bike towards us. In minutes he met us.

"It was getting late, so I thought I'd come and meet you," he said.

Saved! On the bike we could be there in time. Good thinking, Robert!

101

"Late for what?" Claudia asked.

Uh-oh!

Robert looked at me. He hadn't realized I wasn't going to tell Claudia. "Oh, I thought we'd be finished much earlier," I said, trying to make it sound as if it was no big deal. "So I told Robert I'd meet him later, so that we could—"

"So that's why you've been rushing me all evening!" Claudia cried angrily. "And I actually thought you wanted to spend some time with me. Boy, am I a jerk!" Claudia stormed off down the boardwalk.

"You're not a jerk," I said, running after her. "I *did* want to spend time with you. It's just that I thought I could—"

"Save it," Claudia snapped at me. "From now on I'm not talking to you. Not ever!"

With a quick, apologetic glance at Robert, I hurried after Claudia all the way to the house. As we drew close, she broke into a run. I ran behind her, and followed her inside.

Claudia went straight into our room and began gathering up her clothes from the chest of drawers and cupboards. "What are you doing?" I asked.

"I'm moving into the other bedroom," she said, pushing past me, with clothes

102

tumbling from her arms. "I don't want to spend another minute with you."

She went into the room and slammed the door.

9th CHAPTER

Thursday

Jessi, Mal, what is going on with Haley and Vanessa? When I sat for Haley and Matt today, Haley said it all started in camp, over a bathing suit. I asked her to explain, but all she would tell me was, "Vanessa started it, and she's a jealous, know-it-all, spoiled brat, traitor, creep." Then she spent the rest of the day plotting ways to ruin Vanessa's life!

104

Poor Mary Anne! She was completely in the dark about the Vanessa–Haley feud when she went to sit for the Braddocks that afternoon. "Hi, Haley," she said brightly as she came in the door. Then she signed "hi" to Matt, who is profoundly deaf.

Matt smiled and signed "hi" in reply before he turned back to the closed-captioned episode of *Where in the World Is Carmen Sandiego?* he was watching on TV.

Haley hardly seemed to notice Mary Anne. She didn't even look up from whatever she was making on the living room floor.

"She's been working on some top-secret project ever since she came home from day camp this afternoon," said Mrs Braddock. "She won't even let me see what she's writing."

Mary Anne noticed that Haley had draped herself in front of the paper she was working on. Mrs Braddock told Mary Anne that she was meeting Mr Braddock at his office, and they would be going to see a film together. "We shouldn't be later than nine o'clock," she said. "We'll be at the Washington Mall multiplex if you need us."

"All right," said Mary Anne. "Have fun."

When Mrs Braddock had gone, Mary Anne knelt down next to Haley. With her mother gone, Haley was less guarded with her work. She sat up and stretched. When she moved off her paper, Mary Anne couldn't believe her eyes! In red crayon, Haley had written: *Beware of Vanessa Pike. If you are friends with her she will stab you in the back*. Haley had done a drawing of a hand holding up a bloody knife. Mary Anne noticed that behind Haley were about ten other similar drawings. "What are you planning to do with those?" she asked.

"Hang them up all over the neighbourhood," Haley replied. "The other kids need to be warned about Vanessa."

The Pikes live just a few houses away from the Braddocks, on the same side of the street. Mary Anne knew Vanessa was bound to see the signs. "Why are you so angry with Vanessa?" she asked. That was when Haley told her the part about Vanessa being *a jealous, know-it-all, spoiled brat, traitor, creep*.

Haley gathered up her home-made posters and began searching the house for drawing pins. "Haley, you can't hang those up," Mary Anne protested. "They'll embarrass Vanessa and hurt her feelings."

106

"So?" Haley replied. "She embarrassed *me* and hurt *my* feelings. She made me look so stupid by having the same swimsuit. Nobody knows that *she* copied me."

"I bet it was an accident," said Mary Anne. "When did all this start?"

"*She* started it on Monday, and she's been acting like a creep ever since." Haley found a box of drawing pins in a kitchen drawer.

"Haley, friends fight sometimes. It happens. But it will pass and you'll make up," said Mary Anne. "Why don't we put your signs away and play Cluedo," Mary Anne suggested, trying to distract Haley. She knew Haley loved playing Cluedo.

It almost worked. Haley stacked her papers on the kitchen worktop and looked thoughtful. Then the doorbell rang. When Mary Anne peeped out, she couldn't see anyone. Then she opened the door, looked down and saw Pow, the basset hound the Pikes had adopted when the Barrett family could no longer keep him. (Marnie Barrett had developed an allergy to the dog.)

Looking all around, Mary Anne thought she saw something move at the corner of the house. She was sure she heard giggling.

"Pow's got something round his neck,"

said Haley, coming up behind Mary Anne.

Sure enough, Pow was wearing a collar with a cardboard tube attached to it – you know, the way a cartoon St Bernard dog wears a little barrel. *Open this* was written on the tube in blue felt-tip pen. Mary Anne yanked on the piece of orange thread holding the tube to Pow's collar. She pulled off the top. As she did, three red, white and blue accordion-pleated strips of paper jumped out of the tube.

"Ahhh!" Mary Anne cried, startled. She jumped back and dropped the tube. An index card fell out of the tube on to the floor. Mary Anne picked it up. "It says, 'Haley, please—'" She cut herself off when she saw the rest of the message.

Haley grabbed the card from her and read it out loud. "Haley, please wash daily. Because we think you really stink! Help save our neighbourhood from horrible odour. Signed, CASH – Citizens Against Stinky Haley."

Mary Anne sprinted towards the corner of the house, in time to see Vanessa, Nicky and Margo Pike dashing away, with Pow in tow.

"This is war!" Haley announced dramatically. She stomped back to the kitchen and grabbed her pile of papers.

108

"I'll be back soon," she said, heading for the door.

"No!" Mary Anne said. She didn't know what to do. She couldn't let Haley paper the neighbourhood with anti-Vanessa signs. "Haley, don't stoop to her level," she said.

Haley frowned. "What does that mean?"

"It means that just because she's being silly and hurtful, you don't have to be."

"Why not?"

Mary Anne sighed thoughtfully. "Because . . . because . . . it's not a nice way to be."

"I'm not in a nice mood," Haley said firmly, heading for the door again.

"Haley, you need a permit!" Mary Anne said desperately.

"What?"

"You need a permit to hang up signs in Stoneybrook. If you put up those signs, a police officer will come and tell you to take them all down and maybe even make your parents pay a fine. I don't think they'd like that very much."

"You're right," Haley agreed. "They wouldn't. OK, I won't put up my signs all over town. I'll be right back."

"Where are you going?" Mary Anne

called after Haley as Haley ran out of the front door.

Haley ran back. "I'm going to pin these to the Pikes' fence," she said and then ran off again.

Mary Anne let her go. It was better than having her plaster the signs all around the neighbourhood. "Just one sign," she shouted after Haley. "Put up just one."

Sitting on the front step, Mary Anne waited for Haley to return. Matt came out and sat next to her. Matt signed, "Vanessa and Haley are fighting."

Mary Anne nodded. "Why?" she signed back.

Matt shrugged.

Once again, Mary Anne heard a sound from the side of the house. She got up and tiptoed over to investigate. Adam Pike nearly knocked her over as he was sneaking away from the house. "What's going on?" Mary Anne demanded.

Adam went pale. "Er . . . I was . . . er . . . delivering a message for Vanessa."

"Show it to me," said Mary Anne.

"It's by the back door," Adam said quickly, and streaked off across the lawn.

Mary Anne went around to the back. By now Matt had come to see what was going on. On the back steps was a shoe

110

box. Remembering the paper springs, Mary Anne opened it cautiously. Inside were a lot of torn-up papers. Looking closer, Mary Anne realized it was a torn birthday card, a ripped-up photo and a shredded letter.

Mary Anne pieced together the photo. It was easy to see that it had been a Polaroid picture of Haley and Vanessa at a school picnic. Their arms were around one another and they were all smiles. The inside of the birthday card said, "Friends 4-ever, Love, Haley." And the letter was one Haley had sent Vanessa when she went on holiday.

What a shame! thought Mary Anne. How could such good friends become such terrible enemies?

At that moment, Haley came stomping across the lawn. Her fists were clenched at her sides and her face was pink with fury. She was also soaking wet! "What happened?" Mary Anne asked.

"Vanessa saw me putting the signs on her fence and threw water bombs at me from her bedroom window," Haley spluttered. "Her brothers must have helped her fill them up because she had tons of them." Haley touched Matt on the arm. "Come on, Matt," she signed furiously. "Vanessa isn't the only one whose brother can help her. I've got a job for you to do."

Mary Anne hurried after them as they went into the house. What could happen next? Would this feud *ever* end?

10th CHAPTER

Needless to say, Robert and I didn't make it to the sunset sail. By the time I gave up trying to persuade Claudia to open the bedroom door and talk to me, it was eight-forty-five. We'd missed the boat.

When I went back outside, Robert was waiting. "What a mess!" I sighed.

"Want to go for a walk on the beach?" Robert asked sympathetically.

I nodded. He walked his bike as we went along the boardwalk. Off in the distance, I heard a seagull shriek. I had plenty on my mind, but nothing to say. Robert was silent, too.

When we neared the beach, Robert leaned his bike against a tree and I slipped off my sandals. We walked on to the sand, just in time to catch the last of the sunset. "Sorry about missing the sail," I said.

113

"Sorry for turning up like that," Robert replied. "I didn't know it was a secret."

"I should have told you," I said. We held hands and walked with our feet in the surf. After a while, a fat full moon appeared in the sky, out over the water. It was very romantic but I was too upset about what had happened with Claudia to enjoy it much. Still, if I was going to feel miserable, at least I had Robert to feel miserable with.

Up ahead, I saw another couple walking along hand in hand. It was hard to see more than their dark silhouettes in the deep bluish dusk, but I could see they were heading towards us. The man stopped to kiss the woman, then they continued.

I looked out to the ocean. The waves crashed steadily, sending spray into the air. I wondered if I was to blame for what had happened with Claudia. I was only trying to keep her happy by spending time with her. It wasn't my fault everything had gone wrong. I hadn't meant to hurt her feelings. I'd *cared* about her feelings. That's why I was in this mess to begin with.

"What are you thinking?" Robert asked.

I turned to answer him – but I was

114

unable to speak. My jaw just hung open.

"Stacey, what's wrong?" Robert asked urgently.

"That's my father," I managed to say, despite my shock. Dad was only a couple of metres away from us. And he wasn't alone. He was walking hand in hand on the beach with some woman I had never seen before! He and she – whoever she was – were the couple who were walking towards us on the beach!

Just then, Dad spotted me, too. His shoulders stiffened and he stopped short. For a moment, he turned as if he wanted to run away. He didn't, though. He kept coming towards us. What else could he do?

"Stacey!" he said. Although he said my name, he was staring at Robert. Dad couldn't take his eyes off him.

"Hi, Dad . . . this is my . . . friend. . ."

Robert put out his hand to shake. I suppose he wanted to make a good first impression. "Hello, sir. I'm Robert Brewster. It's nice to meet you at last."

Now Dad was shaking Robert's hand but looking at me. "Is this *the* Robert?"

"Well, yes," I had to admit. "Who's *your* friend?"

"This is my . . . er . . . this is Samantha Young." The woman smiled politely, but

115

her expression was uneasy. She was very beautiful, with large blue eyes, thick, wavy brown hair and a great figure. She was wearing a gauzy flower-print skirt, a crocheted top and big, gold hoop earrings. In her hand dangled a pair of gold sandals.

"Did you two meet here on the island?" I asked.

Dad blushed. He actually went red! "Your father and I know one another from the city," Samantha answered for him.

"I see," I said. "And did you just *happen* to run into each other here?"

"No," said Dad, starting to sound a bit annoyed. "Did you and Robert just *happen* to run into one another?"

"No," I replied. Dad and I stood glaring at one another.

At last Dad turned to Samantha. "Would you mind if we call it a night?" he asked. "I think my daughter and I have some things to discuss."

"That's all right," said Samantha. "I'll phone you tomorrow. I suppose that's OK now."

"Of course," said Dad, blushing again. "Come on, Stacey."

"I'll see you tomorrow," I told Robert. "I'm sorry about this – about everything."

116

"No problem," Robert said. "Nice to meet you, Mr McGill, Miss Young."

Dad mumbled something to Robert, and beckoned to me to follow him. He didn't say a word till we were home. Just inside the front door, he stopped and turned towards me. "So, let's hear it. What's going on? How did Robert get here?"

There was nothing to do now but tell the truth. So I did. As I spoke, I could tell Dad was getting angrier and angrier. "Why are you so annoyed?" I asked.

"You used me, Stacey," Dad said, folding his arms. "You took advantage of my offer to spend holiday time together so that you could see your boyfriend. I suppose you've been seeing him behind my back since we arrived. Was Claudia in on this from the start?"

"No," I said. "I didn't tell her about Robert till we got here."

"Oh, very nice," Dad said disgustedly. "You duped your best friend as well. What has she been doing while you've been sneaking off to meet your boyfriend?"

"Just hanging around," I said.

"Oh, how nice for her," he said in the same tone.

"Well, what about you?" I challenged

117

him. "What's Stu Majors been doing while you've been sneaking off to see your girlfriend?"

"Stu has his own life to lead. He wasn't counting on me to spend time with him."

"Maybe not, but you've been lying to *me* since we arrived, haven't you?" I accused him. "All that time you said you were with Mr Majors, you were really with Samantha."

"That's different. I didn't want to upset you. After all, Sam is the first woman I've dated since your mother and I got divorced. I wanted to break it to you gently. I would have introduced you to her before the holiday was over."

"I bet!" I sneered.

"Don't be cheeky, Anastasia," Dad snapped.

"I'm not being cheeky. You get angry with me. You embarrass me in front of Robert. You make me feel terrible, but what I've done is nothing compared with you. How did you get her here, anyway?"

"Stu pulled some strings and found a place for her to rent," he mumbled.

"What if I'd wanted to go to Paris?" I shouted. "Would you have found a place in Paris? Or in Montana? Maybe she'd have been camping out in Cinderella's castle if we'd gone to Disneyland!"

118

"Watch that tone of voice," Dad warned. "For your information, I was originally going to go on holiday with Samantha. Alone – just her and me. But then I realized that I really wanted to spend time with you too. And I worked things out so that I could do both. I did a lot of arranging and spent a lot of money so that I could have this time with you."

"You mean so you could have time with Samantha," I shot back.

"I could have spent it with Sam very easily, without going through all this," he replied angrily.

I turned away from him. I didn't want to hear any more. Hot tears sprang to my eyes. How could my father have lied to me like this? He was carrying on this whole secret life right under my nose. It was as if I didn't even know him.

"Stacey," Dad began. "Listen –"

"Don't speak to me," I cried, pushing past him towards the stairs. "I'm not talking to you."

11th CHAPTER

Friday

Hi, Jessi!

I'm writing this down at the dock. It's early and I just now waved goodbye to Robert as he went off to work. Kristy, Mary Anne and Shannon are due in on the late afternoon ferry. I'm really looking forward to seeing them. I'm looking forward to seeing you and Mal, too, in about a week.

Love,
Stacey

P.S. How's the Haley-Vanessa fight going?

120

What I'd written was true. I couldn't *wait* for Kristy, Mary Anne and Shannon to arrive. I was looking forward to having some company. Claudia wasn't speaking to me. And I had no wish even to see my father.

When I woke up, I saw that the weather fitted my mood perfectly – the sky was dark, and heavy with thunderclouds. It was the first rainy day we'd had since we arrived, and it was fine by me. I pulled on a pair of jeans, a denim shirt and a sweater and headed out to meet Robert.

While walking Robert to the ferry, I told him what had happened with my dad the night before. "I'm sorry you had to find out about Samantha that way," he said. "But I suppose your father was shocked at seeing me, too."

"Please," I groaned. "It is *not* the same thing."

"Samantha seems pretty nice," he said. "She and I walked part of the way home together. She felt bad about what had happened."

"I don't even want to hear that name," I said. "The thought of my dad having a girlfriend is too weird."

When Robert had got on the ferry, I bought postcards and sat by the ferry dock writing them. That took half an hour.

121

Then I bought myself a roll for breakfast. Eating that on the ferry dock took up another fifteen minutes. After that, I leafed through a fashion magazine. By the time I'd read the articles, done the personality quiz and finished the crossword, the ferry was pulling back into the harbour.

"Stacey, have you been here the whole time?" Robert asked when he met me on the dock.

"How could you tell?" I asked.

"I don't know. I just had a feeling."

"I can't bear to go back to that house," I told him.

Robert shook his head sadly. "I feel as if this is my fault."

"No, it's not. And it's not my fault either. If Claudia wasn't so pigheaded and selfish everything would be fine. And if my dad wasn't such a sneak things would be fine with him, too."

"I don't know," said Robert. "That sounds a bit harsh. You know, maybe if you had just—"

"Robert!" I cried, cutting him off. "Whose side are you on?"

"I'm on your side, Stacey. One hundred per cent."

"I know," I said, leaning against him.

"Oh! Here are Claudia's pictures," he said, reaching into the front zip pocket of

122

his mac. "They came in along with my friend's photos – the guy who had them developed for me – so he brought them to me this morning." Robert took three packets of photos out. Two of them were torn open. "The guy ripped them open by mistake," Robert explained. "He thought they were his."

If they hadn't already been open I wouldn't have looked at them. But it was too tempting not to take a look. They were Claudia's sandcastle pictures, and they were *so* beautiful. Real works of art.

The photos reminded me of all the unique, creative things I love about Claudia. Some of the many qualities I would miss if we were never friends again.

Never friends again? Was that possible? I pushed the idea from my brain. I couldn't think about it now.

Half an hour later, Robert went back to work. I had run out of ways to avoid going back, so I walked slowly back to the house. As I'd hoped, Dad had gone out (probably to see Samantha). Claudia was there, though. She had papers spread out on the kitchen table. She was working out the mechanics of her float.

She continued her work without looking at me. I tossed the envelopes with her photos on to the table and went to my

123

room. Plopping down on to the bed, I started reading a Nancy Drew book Claudia had lent me before our fight. (Nancy Drews are her favourites.)

That afternoon, I went down to see Robert twice more. On my second trip, the black clouds let loose a torrent of rain. I had to run back to the house for my red rain poncho. Then I raced down to the dock, splattering through puddles and not stopping till I reached the gangplank.

Robert looked a bit pale when he stepped off the ferry. "What's wrong?" I asked.

"A little seasick, that's all," he answered weakly. "It's pretty rough out there. A lot of passengers were sick."

I pushed his soaking wet hair back from his forehead. "Will they cancel the ferry?"

"Not unless the storm gets a lot worse." He looked at the sky. "Which it might do."

"I hope Kristy, Shannon and Mary Anne can make it across. They're due on the next ferry."

"I hope so too." He took my hand. "Come on, let's get out of this rain. I'm starting to feel waterlogged."

We waited in the doorway of the Harbour Store for nearly all of Robert's break time. It was quite nice being there

124

together in the rain. Mitch, the ferry crew member I'd met, walked by and grinned from underneath his yellow raincoat hood.

"Are we going back out?" Robert asked.

"Of course we are." Mitch laughed. "This is nothing. We've gone out in hurricanes."

Robert swallowed hard. "A hurricane might be better than that constant slow rocking. I've never felt so sick. I didn't even know I got seasick till today."

Mitch laughed. "Come on, Robert. Back to work. We'll make a sailor out of you yet."

Looking even paler, Robert turned to wave to me before he went off with Mitch. I walked home in the rain. In the kitchen, Dad was talking on the phone to someone from the office. "Just fax that stuff to them, and that should do it," he was saying. Claudia was still working silently on her plans.

Dad rang off and turned to Claudia. "How's it going?" he asked her.

"OK, but I don't know why I'm bothering," she replied. "If this weather keeps up there won't be a parade."

It was as if I hadn't even come in. Both of them were ignoring me. I noticed that

Claudia had looked through her photos. The third packet, which I hadn't seen, was lying open. On the top was a picture of Claud and me, posed next to a sand castle. Claudia had mounted the camera on a beach chair, then reached out and clicked the shot. It was a good picture. Just by looking at it, anyone could tell that we were close friends.

Were close friends.

Soon it was time to go down to the dock to meet Shannon, Mary Anne and Kristy. It was raining outside so I grabbed my poncho and went out. I passed Claudia on my way through the kitchen. "I'm going to the dock to meet Kristy and everyone. Come if you want," I said.

Without a word, Claudia stood up and went to her room.

I pulled the red truck off the porch to carry suitcases and began walking towards the dock. I was just one house away when Claudia came out of our house, pulling on her zebra-striped mac. She didn't even look at me, so I didn't wait for her. We walked all the way to the dock that way – me about three houses ahead all the time. Every once in a while I would peep over my shoulder at her, and Claudia would look away sharply.

We were nearly at the dock when the

126

sky opened up completely. It looked as though the rain was being thrown down from the sky in buckets. I started to run, and so did Claudia. At last I reached the dock. The ferry wasn't there.

Splashing through puddles, I ran to the Harbour Store. "Where's the boat?" I asked.

The young woman behind the counter looked up at me. "There's a storm and the water's rough," she said, as if the answer should have been obvious. "They'll be delayed."

"The ferry will be late," I snapped at Claudia as she made her way into the shop. I decided to stand in the doorway and wait.

Claudia moved away from the doorway. I peered around the corner of the shop and watched her make her way towards the Beach Glass Gallery.

For about ten minutes, I waited in the doorway, watching the rain. Then I heard the ferry horn blare. In the next instant, the *Kiki* appeared through the grey mist and driving rain.

I waited for the boat to dock before leaving the shelter of the doorway. Claudia must have heard the ferry horn too, because she appeared on the board-walk just then, heading for the ferry.

I looked for Robert, but didn't see him. Then I remembered he sometimes took a break at this time of day. He'd probably stayed on the Patchogue side. *Good*, I thought. If my friends hadn't spotted him yet, I'd get to tell my side of the story before they asked Claudia a million questions.

We stood a few metres apart and watched the passengers come off. Kristy was the first of our friends to appear. She wasn't smiling. Never before had I seen someone actually look green. But I'm not kidding, her face was a sickly, greyish olive colour.

"Kristy!" I yelled happily.

She nodded at me and gave a small wave. I ran to her and took the canvas bag she was dragging behind her. "I have never felt so sick in my whole life," she muttered as a greeting.

Claudia had joined us. "Where are the others?" she asked.

"Mary Anne and Shannon are still waiting in the queue to get off the boat," said Kristy.

At that moment thunder cracked so loudly we all jumped. A jagged line of lightning split the sky, all the way down into the bay.

Shannon and Mary Anne appeared on the deck then. Both of them were ashen.

128

They smiled weakly. "I've never been so happy to get off a boat," said Shannon when she reached us.

"Put your stuff in here," I said pointing to my truck. I'd brought an extra poncho with me to throw over the bags. I spread it out over the bags. Then we began walking away from the boat.

The rain had let up just a little. Still, it was hard to do much more than walk, with our heads down against the rain. Shannon, Kristy and Mary Anne were still recovering from the trip anyway.

We reached the house at last, and everyone peeled off their wet gear. Dad came in from the main room when he heard us. "Hi, girls," he greeted them. "Don't panic. This is the first bad day we've had. I hope it will be the only one."

"We're not worried," said Shannon. "This place looks wonderful. You lot must be having a great time."

"*Some* people are," said Claudia meaningfully.

"Claudia, why don't you show the girls their rooms?" Dad suggested. Kristy shot me a questioning look. She'd picked up on the fact that Dad hadn't asked *me* to show the rooms.

"Someone can share with me," Claudia said as she headed for the bedrooms.

"And two of you can share a room. That way no one will have to sleep in *her* room."

I stood in the kitchen, stunned at Claudia's rudeness. Dad glanced at me. For a moment I thought I saw a flicker of sympathy in his eyes. But maybe I'd just imagined it. Abruptly, he turned and left.

Thank goodness Kristy, Shannon and Mary Anne were here at last. At least I'd have three friends to talk to.

I went to find them. I was going to say someone *could* share with me, despite Claudia's plans. At the top of the stairs, I saw the door to Claudia's room standing open. Drawing nearer, I could see all four girls inside. Their backs were turned to me.

I could also hear what Claudia was saying. "If I was drowning and it was time for the ferry, she'd probably just let me drown. She won't be wasting time with us if she can be seeing Robert instead, that much I can tell you for sure."

I must have made some noise, because they all turned round suddenly. Claudia looked down at the floor. Shannon, Kristy and Mary Anne just looked at me, their eyes filled with questions.

There goes my chance to tell my side of the story first! I thought.

130

12th CHAPTER

Saturday, July 4

Dear Mallory,

Hi. Happy Fourth of July! We just finished marching in the Fourth of July parade. You should have seen the costumes people wore. Some were really funny. As you know, our friends are here (wish you and Jessi were, too). How are things going at day camp? See you soon.

Love, Stacey

131

The Fourth of July was one of the most bizarre days of my life. It started with Claudia insisting that we all get up early to go down to the soggy beach and build a huge sandcastle on an old piece of plywood she'd found.

To be honest, Claudia didn't insist that *I* join them. She was still acting as though I weren't alive. (So was my father.) But I went along anyway. I wasn't going to stay at home alone and act like some kind of outcast.

Pulling a small convoy of red trucks behind us, we splashed through puddles on our way down to the beach. Claudia had managed to borrow three trucks, one from Mr Majors, one from our neighbours and one from Samantha, and she had the one which came with our beach house, too. Each of us held a truck while Claudia struggled with her large sheet of plywood.

It had stopped pouring, but it was still overcast. "I don't think they'll even have the parade in this weather," said Kristy. "Look at the sky."

"It might clear up," Mary Anne said.

Kristy gave her a small shove on the arm.

"But, er, they'll probably cancel the parade anyway." Mary Anne quickly changed her opinion.

132

"Definitely," added Shannon. "I think we should just forget the whole thing."

Claudia stopped. Resting her plywood on the boardwalk, she studied our friends' faces with a frown. "Don't you lot want to be in the parade?"

"Not really," Kristy admitted.

"Why not?" Claudia cried.

"Well, aren't we rather old for costumes and parades and all that?" Mary Anne said. "I feel a bit daft dressing up as a princess."

"Being a princess isn't so bad!" I said. "What about *my* costume?"

Claudia glared at me, but I didn't care. My costume was the most ridiculous of all.

That morning, Claudia had tossed a green dragon costume on to my bed. It was made out of her green jumpsuit. She'd taped triangular green spikes to the back; leading all the way down to a spiky tail made from Claudia's green scarf. My dragon headpiece was a green Peter Pan hat Mary Anne had borrowed from the Pikes (left over from a Hallowe'en past). It, too, had been adorned with spikes. Shannon had brought a pair of mittens with felt claws attached to the fingertips. (They were the remains of a school play

133

in which she had starred as a lion.) They were part of my costume, too.

I'm sure that casting me as the evil dragon was a not-very-subtle dig from Claudia. I probably should have thrown the stupid costume right back in her face. But I didn't want to be left out.

"Hey, everyone!" Claudia whined. "I've been working on this project for days. You can't back out now."

"Oh, all right!" Kristy gave in. "I suppose we can't say no after all the work you've done."

"*And* we dragged all that costume stuff with us," added Shannon. "We might as well use it."

"I'm still praying for rain, though," Kristy murmured as we continued.

She didn't get rain. All she got was mist, fog, greyness and a bit of drizzle. Just enough to make the day depressing and the sand wet.

Claudia put down the board, and on top of it we tried to recreate the castle she'd sketched. At first, the wet sand looked just right. But we soon saw that it didn't hold together. Or maybe the castle Claudia wanted was too large to be made of sand. Whatever the reason, it wouldn't stay stuck together. No sooner had we built a tower than the base would slide

134

out from under it, or a big crack would appear down the side.

Claudia had made a lot of colourful flags for the castle, out of sticks and brightly coloured construction paper. But every time she poked one in the sand, that part of the castle would crumble.

"This isn't working. Maybe we should just forget the whole thing," said Kristy hopefully.

"I'm not giving up," Claudia insisted. She went to the water's edge and grabbed two fistfuls of seaweed. Working quickly, she poked seaweed into all the cracks until the castle was sealed together. "There," she said, satisfied. "That will hold it."

We picked up the board and loaded it on to the four trucks, which Claudia had tied together with rope. Pulling the float off the beach was nearly disastrous. For one thing, it was heavy. Nearly a metre high and a metre wide, the castle was solid, wet sand. And every time we hit a bump, some of it crumbled. By the time we reached the boardwalk, Claudia had to do some more seaweed patching. But, walking at a snail's pace, we eventually pulled and pushed our gigantic sandcastle to the house in one piece.

"It's nearly time," Claudia said as we

135

parked our castle and went in. She meant time to put on our ridiculous costumes. Mary Anne was the princess, Shannon was the lady-in-waiting, Kristy was the prince, Claudia was the court jester and, of course, I was the dragon. Even though I felt like an idiot, I had to admit that the others looked good. Between the parts Claudia had devised from her own clothing and the bits and pieces the others had brought, the costumes really came together.

Mary Anne and Shannon were in long gowns with veils. Kristy's prince costume included a crown, a cape and a sword we'd bought when we'd put on a video production of Snow White and the Seven Dwarfs with the kids we sit for. Claudia had on a harlequin-print shirt and bright yellow leggings. From papier-mâché, she'd constructed curly, pointed toes for her trainers. She'd painted her trainers, and the points, yellow so they really looked like court jester shoes. She'd used cardboard to make a matching hat.

We were all assembling in the kitchen when Dad appeared, dressed in a red, white and blue suit with a bright red bow tie. He was wearing a tall top hat, and his hair was powdered white. "What do you think?" he asked (of everyone but me).

136

"I'm Uncle Sam. My . . . my friend went to Patchogue and rented costumes for us. She's going to be Lady Liberty."

My humiliation was complete.

"We'd better get going," said Dad. I couldn't believe this was *my* father, wasting precious work time, so he could march around in front of a lot of strangers in a stupid costume. And with his new girlfriend!

Didn't he have a fax to send or something? In the past he always had! It suddenly seemed to me that having a father who worked all the time might not be the worst thing in the world. I was starting to miss it.

"See you down at the parade," Dad said cheerily.

"Your father's got a friend who's a *she*?" Kristy asked, when Dad had walked out of the door.

"Don't remind me," I said.

"She's very nice," Claudia said in a huffy voice. "I spoke to her on the phone and she seemed extremely sweet. When I asked to borrow her truck for this float she sent it over with Mr McGill that very night."

Right then I wanted to hit Claudia over the head with her jester's stick. (Which was artistically rendered from a thin tree

137

branch wrapped in colourful hair ribbons.)

"Let's go," said Claudia. By the time my tail and I made it through the door, Dad wasn't in sight. He'd probably dashed off to meet his new love, Lady Liberty.

Claudia and Kristy took hold of the front truck handles. Shannon and Mary Anne pushed, with the handles in the rear, and our float began rolling towards the dock with me – the dragon – trudging along behind.

All the entrants were assembling down by the dock. The parade would march along the bay side, and then back.

I looked over the crowd and spotted Dad and Samantha. She looked completely gorgeous in a flowing white gown strapped over one shoulder. Perched on her brown wavy hair was a Statue of Liberty crown, and she was holding a torch. Dad was gazing at her with so much admiration you'd think she really was the Statue of Liberty come to life.

I was relieved to hear the blast of the ferry horn as the *Kiki* pulled away from the dock. At least Robert wouldn't see me looking so absurd in this costume.

The parade began promptly at noon. In spite of the weather, a lot of people came out to see it. There was a wide variety of costumes. Three guys were dressed as the tattered soldiers of The Spirit of '76. One woman turned up in a red sequinned baton-twirler's outfit with a big headdress made from shimmering gold and silver metallic streamers. A sash across her costume read: Miss Firecracker. A man on stilts was dressed as Abraham Lincoln.

Ours wasn't the only beach theme. There was a girl dressed as *The Little Mermaid*, marching with her father, who was in costume as King Triton. Another couple were Popeye and Olive Oyl.

As we marched by I heard people ooh and ahh at our costumes. Claudia smiled smugly. (Any other day I would have said she smiled proudly or happily. But today her smile looked so self-satisfied and smug I couldn't stand it.)

"Girls!" called a voice from the crowd, "Castle float!" Kristy, Claudia and Mary Anne stopped to see who had called. Shannon and I didn't stop as quickly. The castle wobbled as our trucks collided with one another. I spotted the caller, a woman with a camera slung around her neck. She ran towards us. "I'm from the paper. Can I get a picture?"

Oh, no! If this were in the paper, Robert was sure to see it.

"Get in close to your sand castle," the woman instructed. "Now smile."

But instead of smiling, we all gasped in horror as our sand castle chose that moment to slide on to the ground.

"Oh, well!" the woman laughed nervously as she went on to photograph some other marchers.

"That's it!" Claudia shouted. "I've had it!" She stomped off angrily, leaving the rest of us to cope with the heap of sand.

Kristy sighed deeply as she lifted the plywood off the trucks and leaned it against a tree. "I feel as though we've walked into a war zone around here. I've never seen Claudia so upset."

"Poor Claudia," said Mary Anne, beginning to load the wet sand into a truck.

"Poor Claudia?" I yelped. Had they thought I wasn't listening? "What about me? I'm the one no one is talking to!"

"That *is* sort of your own fault, don't you think?" said Kristy, in her usual blunt way.

"Not at all!" I snapped.

We picked up most of the sand, and brushed the rest to the side. We didn't bother to finish the parade; we trudged home instead. It was just as well. As we reached the house, it started to rain again.

The rest of that day and Sunday were simply awful. The weather was miserable. Dad and Claudia still wouldn't speak to me, except through one of the others. ("Kristy, please ask Stacey to pass the meatballs." "Shannon, would you ask Stacey where she put my green scarf.") Shannon, Kristy and Mary Anne didn't seem to know what to do. It was hard for them, being caught in the middle between Claudia and me. Claudia and I were both miserable, too.

Shannon, Kristy and Mary Anne amused themselves by going for walks in the rain, playing cards and reading. Claudia and I didn't join them in much of it, because it meant we'd have to be together.

For all those reasons, the beach house felt unbearably small that weekend. The only breaks I got were when I went to meet Robert. Even he seemed to be in a crummy mood, though. Maybe it was the after-effects of being out on the rolling sea all day. Maybe it was the gloomy weather. But he definitely wasn't himself.

Luckily, on Monday morning the sun was back. At least my friends would have one great beach day before they left on Tuesday. Seeing the sun really brightened my mood. I sprang out of bed and hurried

141

into the hall. "Hey, everyone, beach weather!" I called, ready to make a fresh start on the holiday. I'd decided not to meet Robert for work. I was going to spend all of this last day with my friends.

Mary Anne opened the door of the bedroom she was sharing with Shannon. She and Shannon were already dressed. I was surprised to see their suitcases open on the beds. "You're leaving?" I asked.

"We thought it would be best to get going," said Shannon, looking uncomfortable.

That really put a dent in my make-everything-better plans! Though I suppose I shouldn't have been completely surprised. Between the weather and the tension in the house, it couldn't have been the greatest holiday they'd ever had.

Just then, the door to Claudia and Kristy's room opened. Kristy came out with her suitcase. "Thanks for having us, Stacey," she said. "It's a long journey. We wanted to get started."

"It's such a nice day, though," I said. Then my jaw dropped, as Claudia came out holding *her* suitcase. "*You're* leaving too?" I cried. "You were supposed to stay till next Saturday and then go home with Dad and me."

Claudia shot me a Look. The look said:

142

Are you stupid? Don't you know why I'm leaving?

Honestly, I didn't blame her. The holiday had been a disaster for her too.

They didn't even stop for breakfast. I walked with them as they hurried down to the ferry. "'Bye, everyone," I said as they walked up the gangplank.

"'Bye, Stacey," said Shannon, "Enjoy the rest of your holiday.

"Thanks." I could see Robert now, looking down at us from the top deck. I hoped he'd come down. I needed a friendly face and a hug right then. He didn't come down, though. He just waved, and he wasn't smiling.

Unexpectedly, tears started to well up in my eyes. How had everything turned into such a mess?

13th CHAPTER

Monday

The Vanessa-Haley feud is driving me nuts! Jessi and I can't take one more day of bickering, mean notes, and shouting. It's practically ruined our day camp job. So we've come up with a plan to bring them back together.

144

Mallory wrote that in the club notebook during the Monday meeting. Even though Kristy, Shannon, Mary Anne and Claudia only got back from Fire Island at three-thirty that afternoon, Kristy insisted on holding a regular meeting. (I was the only one missing but I bet my name was mentioned a lot. They probably spent half the meeting discussing what a terrible time they'd had.)

On Tuesday, Mal and Jessi got a chance to try out their plan. By that time, the feud between Vanessa and Haley was over a week old. Something had to be done.

That afternoon, camp was held at a nearby park. The counsellors had planned a field day, with lots of comedy sketches, fun food, games and relay races. All the campers were divided into two huge teams, blue and red. Jessi and Mal made sure Haley and Vanessa were both in the blue team.

Not only that, they made sure that the girls were always together whenever a relay race called for partners. "You've got to be joking!" Vanessa cried when Mal informed her that she and Haley would have to run together in the three-legged race.

"No joke. You're partners," Jessi confirmed.

"I'm changing," Haley declared. She looked around at the other kids. "Who wants to swap and be my partner?" No one said anything. "See?" said Haley, looking at Vanessa. "Everyone would rather die than be your partner."

"Maybe everyone would rather be eaten by a shark than be your partner," Vanessa replied.

"Both of you are big grouches," said a small girl with curly red hair.

"Who asked you?" Vanessa snapped at her.

Mal and Jessi just rolled their eyes.

The plan was to get Vanessa and Haley to work together. If the three-legged race was any indication, the plan was doomed. Just getting Haley and Vanessa's legs tied together was a problem. "Don't even let your leg touch me," Haley commanded.

"Believe me, I don't want the fleas from your leg jumping on to me," Vanessa said.

When it was their turn to run, Haley ran the race on her own, dragging Vanessa along. "Get your legs moving together!" Jessi coached from the sideline.

It wasn't long before Vanessa tumbled right on top of Haley. "Get off me!" Haley screamed. They flailed around like a turtle on its back for a few minutes before righting themselves. By that time,

146

most of the three-legged runners had made it to the finishing line and were handing their ties to the next pair. Haley and Vanessa stumbled along, anxious to catch up but still unable to work together. The blue team lost that event.

The next event was just as bad. Vanessa and Haley were paired again, in a race which required that both partners climb on to a blown-up float, and then co-operate to move it forward, with one paddling in front and one kicking at the back. This was held in the park's large outdoor pool. (By this time, neither girl was wearing a red-striped bathing suit. Both had found substitutes.)

"Move up," Vanessa snarled at Haley as they tried to get into position on the float. "Your big behind is in my face."

"I'm not the one with the big rear end," Haley replied.

They squirmed and argued so much that they were well behind the other floats. In the middle of the pool Vanessa decided Haley was taking up too much of the float, so she tried to push her forward. Haley didn't want to be moved. You can probably guess the rest – both girls tumbled off, and the float drifted away. By the time they retrieved it, they were last once again.

"Do we have to have them on our

team?" asked one of the blue-team kids when the race was over.

"Yeah," agreed the girl with the red curls. "Can we send them over to the reds?"

"Oh, be quiet!" Vanessa and Haley shouted together.

Startled to hear their voices saying the same thing at the same time, they actually looked at one another. "We've got a problem here," said Vanessa to Haley. "Everyone is going to be furious with us if we lose another race as badly as we lost the first two."

Haley nodded. "We have to start working together."

"Just for today, though," Vanessa said cautiously. Mal told me later that when she heard Vanessa and Haley talking like this she felt the first of glimmer of hope. She and Jessi looked at one another and crossed their fingers.

The next event was the back to back crabwalk. Kids had to sit back to back, link arms and then crabwalk to the finishing line together. "Ready?" Vanessa checked with Haley as their turn came up.

"Ready," Haley confirmed. No one could believe the change. Back to back, Haley and Vanessa scrambled to the finishing line like they'd been crabwalking

148

together all their lives. When they started, the blue team had been slightly behind. Vanessa and Haley helped them catch up, and won the relay by a narrow margin.

"Hurrah!" Mallory cheered.

Forgetting themselves, Vanessa and Haley slapped their hands together in the air. Then, suddenly, they remembered their feud and frowned. It didn't matter. Mallory knew that somehow, the line had been crossed. From then on, they couldn't go back to being enemies.

She was right too. Vanessa and Haley triumphed at every event. They went from being the worst to being the stars of the blue team. "Look out, reds!" the curly-haired girl cried during one event. "Here come our secret weapons, Vanessa and Haley!" What a turnaround!

In the end, the blue team won. It wasn't entirely due to Vanessa and Haley, but they were the team heroes anyway.

As the kids prepared to perform a comedy sketch about camp life, Jessi and Mallory complimented themselves on their brilliant plan. "We just found a quality both of them have in common," said Jessi.

"I know," Mal agreed. "They're both super-competitive – which is one of the reasons why they got into the whole swimsuit feud in the first place. Each one

149

wanted to be the first to have chosen the suit. And they each wanted everyone else to know it too."

"But it's also the reason why they're friends," Jessi pointed out. "They've got so much in common."

Just then, Vanessa and Haley came past. Haley was holding a large cardboard tree, a prop for the sketch. "Haley, you'll hurt yourself," said Vanessa. "Let me help you with that tree."

"Oh, no," Haley objected. "You worked hard enough at the relay races. It's thanks to you that we did so well."

"No way," Vanessa insisted as she lifted up the back of the tree for Haley. "You were the one who did most of the work."

"Absolutely not. You were amazing in the water balloon toss," said Haley, seeming to have forgotten that not long ago, she'd been the object of Vanessa's water balloon-throwing skills.

"But you filled the balloons so quickly," Vanessa replied.

As Haley and Vanessa walked off with their cardboard tree, Jessi and Mallory collapsed with laughter. "You realize that they're doing it again, don't you?" said Jessi.

"Doing what?" Mal asked.

150

"Being competitive," Jessi pointed out. "They're competing to see who can be more apologetic and polite."

"You're right," Mallory agreed. "But it's better than the feud. A lot better."

14th CHAPTER

Thursday

Dear Claudia,

I'm so, so glad we talked on the phone last night. More than anything in the world, I really hope we will be friends again. We can talk more when I get home. I know we still have things to discuss. But at least we're talking again.

Love, Stacey

My second week on Fire Island just kept getting worse and worse. My friends had gone. Dad made a few meals and always let me know where he would be, but things weren't the same between us. We were still angry with one another. Then to top it all, Robert starting acting more and more strangely towards me.

He'd tell me he had to stay on the boat and do some extra work when I came to meet him. He did that a few times in a row, and then he suggested that I didn't walk him to work in the mornings.

"There's no reason for you to get up so early," he said as we stood off to the side of the boat. I sensed there was more to it than his being concerned about my rest.

"What's wrong?" I asked. "Are you angry with me?"

"No, not angry. Not exactly."

"Then exactly what?"

Robert looked away. "I think maybe we've been spending too much time together. We're quite young, and maybe we should be seeing other people."

At once I felt a burning sensation at the back of my eyes, like I wanted to cry but no tears were coming. "Why do you feel that way?" I asked. "After everything that's happened to me on this holiday, how can you say that?"

"That's why I'm saying it," said Robert. "To tell you the truth, Stacey, the way you've treated everyone makes me uncomfortable."

"The way *I've* treated everyone?"

"Well, yes. The lying and all. Seeing Claudia leaving on Tuesday with your other friends really started me thinking. It bothers me that you kept trying to do things behind everyone's back. I mean, first you didn't tell Claudia I would be here. It wasn't a surprise for her, Stacey, it was a lie. And even after she knew, you kept on lying to her – you didn't even tell her you were meeting me after your dinner that night. Why did that have to be a secret?"

"Because I didn't want to hurt her feelings."

"But you wound up hurting her feelings even more."

"I know," I said. "Don't you think I feel bad about that? I knew she wouldn't understand about my seeing you."

"You didn't even give her a chance," Robert insisted.

"What's the matter with you?" I asked angrily. "Why are you being so hard on me?"

154

"Here's the thing, Stacey. If you would lie to your own father *and* your very best friend, how long before you lie to me?"

"Robert!" I cried, shocked. "I would never lie to you!"

Robert shook his head sadly. "Sorry, Stace, I just don't believe you. The more I think about it, the more it bothers me. What if you decided *I* wouldn't understand something, the way you decided with Claudia and your father. For me to be close to someone, I have to trust that person."

"But you *can* trust me, Robert," I said.

"After what I've learned about you this week, I don't think I can," he said as he turned to walk away.

"You creep!" I cried to his back. "I only lied so I could spend time with you!"

He turned back and looked at me sadly. "I'm sorry, Stacey. I can't change how I feel."

A dozen different feelings swept through me at once. I was furious with him for turning on me like this. He was so ungrateful for what I'd gone through to be with him. Yet I felt guilty too, because what he'd said was true. I had lied. I was ashamed to have my lies laid out for me the way he'd just done. I'd seen myself as clever. I was proud that I'd worked out such a good plan. But in his eyes, I just seemed conniving and sneaky. It was mortifying.

But the worst emotion I felt was loneliness. It was a hollow, empty feeling I'd never truly experienced before. The feeling was so strong it was like a physical pain.

Now the burning sensation in my eyes melted into hot tears. I was utterly, completely miserable.

The *Kiki*'s horn blasted. I looked up in time to see Robert climbing the metal stairs to the upper deck. I suddenly understood why people use the expression heartbroken. There was a feeling inside me so painful it had to be my heart breaking.

I'd once liked an older guy called Wes who just thought of me as a kid. I thought I'd felt bad when I realized he'd never be in love with me. But this was different. It was so much worse. My feelings for Robert were much deeper than some silly crush. I couldn't believe I'd lost him. It was too awful.

With my head down, I turned towards the boardwalk. I wasn't sure where I was going, I just had to walk. I went along the bay and then turned on to one of the side

156

paths. The clear blue sky seemed all wrong. It didn't fit my mood at all.

I wasn't really paying attention to where I was going, so I was surprised when I found myself in front of the Beach Glass Gallery. It was really just a house, with a sign in front. But the front door was open and I was desperate for something to distract me from thinking about Robert, Claudia and my dad. I walked up the wooden steps and went into the gallery.

If I wanted to forget, I'd come to the *wrong* place. There, hanging on the walls, were Claudia's sandcastle photos! They'd been enlarged and given a matt finish, and they took up an entire wall. "Hello. Can I help you?" asked a short woman with frizzy greying hair.

"Where did those photos come from?" I asked, dazed.

"A lovely young artist, around your age, was here about a week ago. She'd come in several times to look at the artwork. One day, a packet of photos fell out of her pocket. These are her photos. I was so struck with them that I offered to mount them for her and show them in my gallery. I've got a price list if you're interested."

"Yes, I am," I said. She handed me a paper with a list of titles: "Claudia's

157

Castle Dreams", "That's the Way the Castle Crumbles", and so on. Claudia was asking twenty dollars apiece for her pictures.

"As a matter of fact," the gallery owner continued, "the artist is on the front page of the paper today."

"She is?" I asked, dazed. This was all so strange. It almost felt like a dream. I went to the counter and looked at the local Fire Island paper. Half the front page was devoted to the parade. There were three pictures, and one of them was of my friends and me looking on in horror as our castle slid away from us. The caption under it read: "Despite some bad weather and minor mishaps, everyone had a great time." (I suppose that was a matter of opinion.)

The gallery owner looked at me. "Why, you're in this picture, too, aren't you?"

I nodded.

"Tell Claudia her photos are receiving a wonderful response," said the gallery owner. "I haven't seen her since I put them up on Monday."

"She went home," I said, my voice quavering. "Excuse me, I have to go." I didn't want to start crying all over everything. The idea that Claudia would have something this exciting happen and not tell me about it was too much.

With tears in my eyes I stumbled out of the gallery. I was cut out of everyone's life now. No one wanted me to be a part of what they did.

Not knowing where else to go, I headed for home. I didn't expect Dad to be there, but he was. He was sitting at the kitchen table reading. He noticed my puffy eyes. "Stacey, what's the matter?" he asked warmly, closing his book.

Those were the first words he'd spoken to me in days. The concern in his voice made me start crying all over again. "Robert's broken up with me, Claudia hates me, you're not speaking to me – everything's horrible," I blurted out.

"I think we'd better talk," Dad said. "Have a seat."

Using a tea towel to dry my eyes, I sat down. "I've been thinking," Dad said. "And I owe you an apology."

"You do?" I questioned.

"I think you owe me an apology, too," he added. "But I've been just as bad. I should have told you about Samantha. I thought I was trying to protect you, but really I was trying to protect myself."

"What do you mean?" I asked.

"I really was planning on telling you

about Samantha, but not till the weekend. You see, I wanted to have at least half the holiday in peace, in case you were upset about Samantha. I told myself I was doing it for your sake. There's never really any good excuse for lying to someone you love, though. Somehow it always winds up making matters worse."

"Mum says you hate talking about difficult things," I remembered.

A sad smile formed on his lips. "She's right. It's always been easier for me to avoid difficult issues than to discuss them. I suppose this is an example of that problem."

"Maybe I'm like you," I said.

"Maybe you are," he agreed. "But it's not a healthy way to be. It doesn't do you any good. All it got me was a divorce. That's not all there was to it, of course, but that trait didn't help me with your mother. She's much more direct."

"I'm sorry about not telling you about Robert," I said. "You're right. I was taking the easy way out. I should have been honest. Would you have minded coming here if I'd told you straight out?"

"I don't know," he admitted. "I'd have appreciated your honesty. I probably would have come around to it."

"And Claudia would have known what

160

she was getting herself into if I'd told her," I said. "She could have chosen."

Dad nodded. "I love you, darling. You'll always be my girl. And life will go on – for both of us," he said, putting his arm around me.

I wiped my tears and smiled a little. "Claudia said Samantha's nice."

"She is," said Dad with a grin. "Tell you what. Why don't you come out to dinner with us tonight? You can start getting to know her."

I wasn't sure I was ready for that. But it felt so good to be talking to Dad again. "All right," I said. "I love you too, Dad."

He reached across and ruffled my hair. "We're some pair, huh?" he said. "Two of a kind."

"Dad, do you think we're sneaky and conniving?" I asked.

He sat back in his chair and crossed his arms thoughtfully. "No," he said after a moment. "I think we don't like confrontation and unpleasantness. It's very tempting to avoid issues when you're like that. But avoidance is a form of lying, and it leads you into real lies. You know, I didn't even realize all that about myself till Samantha pointed it out."

"Want to go down to the beach?" I asked him.

161

"I can't right now," he said. "I'm waiting for Sam to call about tonight. How about if I meet you down there?"

"All right," I agreed.

I changed into my swimsuit, grabbed a towel, and headed out to the boardwalk. Halfway to the beach, I heard footsteps behind me. I turned and saw Robert running towards me. "Stacey, wait!" he called.

I stopped and waited for him to catch up. I spoke first. "Robert, listen. I know I've done some awful things lately. I don't blame you for thinking badly of me. But I've learned my lesson. Really. I don't want to lose you. I promise that you'll never catch me lying to you or anyone else again."

"Thanks. But I was too hard on you," Robert said. "I'm not sure why. Maybe it's because I think of you as perfect. This is the first time I've seen a side of you that isn't . . . well . . . isn't perfect. I'm really sorry."

"You don't want to break up?" I asked hopefully.

"No, no, not at all. I got on the ferry and I realized that that was what I'd done. I hadn't meant to, but somehow it came out sounding like that. When I realized that, I couldn't wait to get back and try

162

to make things right. I ran all the way here."

I threw my arms around him. He hugged me back.

Now there was just one more person I had to make things right with.

"Will you walk me back to the dock?" Robert asked.

"I can't," I said. "I need to make an important phone call." I walked with him as far as our beach house. "Do you want to come out to dinner with my dad, Samantha and me tonight?" I asked.

Robert made a funny, fake-horrified face. "Do I have to?"

"No," I said.

"All right. I will."

I kissed him happily. "I'll meet you when you come in off your last ferry run."

Then I went inside to phone Claudia, and tell her I was sorry.

15th CHAPTER

"Mum!" I cried as I stepped off the train at the Stoneybrook station. She was waiting on the platform. It was so great to see her. I hugged her tightly.

We loaded all my stuff into the car and headed for home. "Would you mind dropping me off at Claudia's?" I asked.

"Stacey, I haven't seen you for two weeks!" Mum objected.

"I won't be there long," I promised. "It's really important that I talk to her."

"I ran into Claudia at the mall," Mum said. "Of course I was surprised to see her, as I thought she was with you. She told me what had happened, but I had the feeling she wasn't telling me everything."

I looked at Mum. Claudia had probably left out the part about Samantha. "She told you about Robert, though, I

164.

suppose," I said, wanting to avoid the Samantha subject myself.

Mum nodded. "You should have been more honest, Stacey."

"I know, believe me!" I said. "I've learned my lesson. That's why I have to go and straighten things out with Claudia in person."

"I understand," said Mum as she pulled up at the kerb in front of Claudia's house.

"Thanks," I said, kissing her cheek before I slid out of the front seat.

Claudia must have spotted the car, because she opened the front door before I even rang the bell. "Hi," I said, feeling a little shy.

"Come on in," Claudia said. We went up to her room and shut the door.

For the first time ever, I felt awkward and out of place in Claudia's room. I stood by the door nervously. "I just want to say that I'll never do anything like that to you – or to anyone – again. I'm really, really sorry," I said. "I hope we can go back to being best friends."

"I hope so too," Claudia agreed seriously.

I nodded and smiled. "Oh, and I've got these for you," I said, pulling a large yellow envelope out of my shoulder bag. In the envelope were two of the photos which had been displayed at the Beach Glass Gallery, three receipts and . . . "There's sixty dollars in there," I told her. "You sold three photos. Dad bought one for Samantha."

"Wow!" said Claudia, taking the envelope. "People actually bought them. I can't believe it. But, you know, I thought they *were* pretty good."

"They're beautiful photographs," I said sincerely.

Claudia folded up the money. "I'm low on babysitting money after taking a week off. This money will buy crisps, art supplies and Nancy Drews."

"That's all you need to be happy," I said.

"No," Claudia said seriously. "I need my best friend, too."

"So do I," I said as I hugged her. "I won't let anything, not even a boy, ever come between us again."

"I've got something for you, too," said Claudia. She opened her top drawer and pulled out the photo of both of us building the sand castle together. It was enlarged and had a matt finish. "Here," she said. "I had this made up for you after you rang on Thursday. I've done some thinking too. I might have overreacted a bit. I could

166

have been more understanding. After all, what are friends for?"

I took the photo from her. On it was written "Friends For Ever by Claudia Kishi".

"Thanks, Claud," I said. "This is the best present in the world."

After that, I had to go home. Mum would be upset if I stayed away too long. Besides, I had missed her too. When I got home, she was weeding her garden, but I knew she was really waiting for me. (Mum only weeds when she's killing time.) "Are you two friends again?" she asked when she saw me coming up the front walk.

"Yup," I said and showed her the photo Claudia had given me.

"That's lovely," said Mum, looking at the photograph. "Stacey, I'm sure Claudia wasn't telling me something," Mum pressed. "What was it?"

I have to admit that my first impulse was to come up with some story. I knew Mum wouldn't want to hear about Samantha. Even though she and Dad are divorced, I think Mum still has a lot of feelings for him. I was sure she wouldn't like the idea of my spending two weeks with a potential stepmother either. (Although Dad told me he and Sam aren't nearly that serious yet.) I was opening my mouth to say that the only thing Claud had left out was that Dad and I had had a little disagreement in the beginning.

Then – thank goodness – I caught myself.

"What she didn't tell you is that Dad has got a new girlfriend, and she was there. Not in our house, but in Davis Park. Dad didn't tell me at first, and we had a big fight over it."

Mum sat back on her heels and absorbed this information. "Did you meet her?"

"Yeah, she's all right."

"Do you feel OK about it?" she asked.

"I didn't at first, but now I do. How about you?"

"It was bound to happen sooner or later," she said slowly. "It will take me a little while to get used to it. Thank you for telling me."

"I thought you should know," I said.

Mum smiled a little. "Yes, I should know something like that."

The rest of Saturday and Sunday passed quietly. I spent most of Sunday evening writing Robert a *long* letter, just sort of going over everything that had happened. After all those rough patches, our double date with Dad and Samantha had gone really well. We all had a good time and started to relax with one another. From then on, the rest of the holiday was great. Spending so much time with Robert was the best. It made me miss him even more now.

By Monday, the whole holiday was starting to seem like something that had happened long ago. I was back at our regular BSC meeting, sitting on Claudia's bed and collecting subs, just like always.

Logan Bruno was there. (He doesn't always come to meetings, but as he was around, he'd decided to drop in.) He was busily reading the club notebook, bringing himself up-to-date. He'd been away (in Louisville, Kentucky, where he used to live), so he wanted to catch up on everything that had been happening while he was away. "Are Vanessa and Haley still friends?" he asked as he closed the book.

"They're such lovey-dovey friends that it's sickening," Mallory told him. "Our day camp job was fun, but I'm glad it's over. For the last few days, they were continually saying stuff like: 'Excuse me, Haley, my most wonderful friend,' 'What, Vanessa, my Number One best bud?' 'Oh, you've smudged your trainer, Haley, allow me to wipe it for you.' It got to be too much after a while."

"At least I can get away from them,"

Jessi laughed. "Mal is stuck with them at her house all summer."

"That's why I'm never at home," Mal said, rolling her eyes.

"Well, if you want to escape from your house, we'll have plenty of work for you," said Kristy." A lot of our customers are coming home from holiday. Our little holiday from babysitting is about to come to an end."

I can't say that made me sad. I'd had about enough of holidays for a while. I was eager for normal life – and that meant being friends with Claudia again. I hope Claudia and I will be friends for ever. And that's no lie!